I0718471

Forbidden & Explicit Sex Stories For Adults:

Taboo Erotica Collection-Gangbangs, BDSM, Rough Anal, Sex Games& Toys, First Time Lesbian, Femdom, Orgasmic Oral& 69, Tantra& More

Written By:

G.G. Goode

Goode Publications

Table of Contents

~CHAPTER 1~

Rough Anal from The Mystery and No Face Man

Subway Sex – A lonely woman introverted and absorbed in her day-to-day life encounters a stranger from behind. He knows her kind. He knows she needs his dick, and he gives it to her. Slowly at first. From behind. She has no idea who he is. She has no control over what he does to her. All she knows is that it feels damned good. The whole time he pleasures her with his fingers she vows to herself that she'll stop before it goes too far. Before she knows it, he's penetrating her virgin ass and she is his, in more ways than one.

~HER~

Everyone around me was living in their own secluded lives. They had their minds in their own fucked up worlds. I knew this because no one in their right mind would ride this subway every day to a job that kept them barely alive in a city you could barely breathe in. New York was supposed to be the city that never sleeps. A city where dreams come true. Such bullshit. I used to think so five years ago when I had my suitcase in my hand, and I left my Kansas home to pursue my dreams.

Now I stand in a crowded subway with my hand clutching a metal pole as it careens me to my job. It was supposed to be temporary. It was only supposed to be a stepping stone. It was supposed to happen for me by now. Instead, I have gotten empty promises and nowhere paths. I felt lost, absorbed, invisible, a permanent part of New York, and I didn't know how to change it.

I gripped the cold metal pole as the train quickly stopped to take on more monotone faces. The car was getting tighter, the crowd around me pushing closer. Someone's elbow pressed into my side. Another body brushed against my back as they pushed past me to fight for the corner of a seat to claim. I used to look up when this happened. A small smile to pass along or an apology as I tried to move out of their way. Now, it's just part of my journey to and from work. As were the lights that constantly flickered threatening to leave us all in the dark on our evening ride.

I moved toward the wall to allow others access, my eyes glued to a woman's face standing on the outside platform. This wasn't her train. She knew this without moving her eyes from her phone. Hers looked much like this one but hers went to another part of the city. She'd know when it arrived. She'd move to board when it was time, her eyes never moving from her phone, absorbed in her own fucked up little world. She dressed much like I did, her skirt to her knees and her long coat dangling off her shoulders. She could be pretty if she'd just smile. She was a permanent part of New York too. I attempted a smile then aborted the mission. Why bother? No one would look. No one would smile back. No one gave a shit.

~HIM~

I was tired of the crowded subway and craved my spacious town car again. I suppose it was the part of me that felt I was better than everyone else, the narcissist in me. I tried working on bettering myself but all of the expensive therapists in the world couldn't help me. I was broken and my family did that to me. Filthy rich and always looking down on everyone, they taught me to live and love for money, not from the heart. My wallet grew, my heart did not. I married for looks and I fucked for dominance, and I didn't care who I hurt in the process. It made me a shell of a man. My supermodel wife left me when she caught me with her sister and her two best friends. A good prenup and a better lawyer left her penniless while I traveled to Bali. Yes, I felt guilty as hell, but not for hurting her. I felt guilty because I didn't feel bad. Does that make sense? I was fucked up but shoved it off by shoving my dick into another sex kitten who wanted to screw a rich man. No feelings, just sex, and greed. They all left when the prenup came up. This was when I knew it all had to change. And I knew what I had to do.

Looking across the empty faces I settled my eyes on her and I watched her. She was my goal. She was my way out of the mental room I locked myself into. I screamed to get out, but no one ever heard me. She'd hear me. She'd feel me. She'd change everything.

Each day I watched her I knew her a little deeper. Each day I learned her rituals, her schedule, her demeanor, and her mind. She became my focus. She needed me as much as I needed her. I just had to prove that to her, and I would. That evening. It was time to make her mine and show her how to break out of her mental room.

~HER~

The train moved slowly at first then as it picked up speed as the landscape rushed past and the lights flickered like a shorted-out strobe light. The scenery out the windows changed quickly, from graffiti walls to busy streets where the last light faded from the day. I leaned my shoulder against the wall and clutched my long coat to my chest, my bare legs a little cold from the December air. The lights went out just as the train went into another tunnel, the car going dark. No one moved. No one cared. It was an everyday occurrence. Cell phones lit up faces. A stranger pressed against my back. I couldn't move forward any further. I didn't think anyone could move anywhere until the train stopped to let some off. I ignored the body behind me until a hand slid up the back of my arm. I turned away slightly, and the hand disappeared. The lights flickered, attempting to illuminate the car again but failed. The hand returned, this time moving along the small of my back. I turned slightly again but the hand stayed. Letting my coat go, I pulled my hand up behind me to shoo the stranger away. His fingers wrapped around my wrist and held me there. My breath caught. I've had incidents before where men have tried to cop a cheap feel, but this was different.

Controlling. Demanding. His body pressed into me pinning my hand between us.

"Shhhhh." The warmth of his breath surrounded my ear.

Chills covered my arms and fed up my back. Part of me prayed for the lights to come back on, but oddly, part of me felt a little heat from this heinous little fantasy. What would it hurt to allow a perfect stranger to touch me inappropriately? As long as it didn't go too far. I relaxed a little.

His grip tightened around my wrist, his other hand trailing around my waist between me and the wall. My coat was pulled open for access and I didn't move when his hand moved across my stomach.

I swallowed hard, a quiver spreading through me and taking control. It pushed a tingling sensation down between my legs.

He gripped my blouse and pulled it from my skirt, before slipping his hand underneath it. The warmth and the strangeness fueled my fire that began the moment he seized my wrist.

I reached back and grabbed his leg. It was firm, muscular, the material of his pants soft to the touch. The moment the lights flickered back on I jumped and pulled my hand away. He did not. I glanced nervously at the others around me, their blank faces still absorbed in their own thoughts. What was happening to me was invisible to them, but it consumed my entire being. This stranger slammed his existence into my life without an invite, without question, and without approval.

"Do not move, my pet." His whisper was close to my ear, and his claim to me excited me. "Let me." He directed me to face the wall and pulled my coat back around me before boxing me in.

My breath was shaky, my hands were cold, my pussy was wet. Excitement radiated through me. I'd allow him to go a little further. He was barely under my clothes. What was the harm?

"I see you," he continued. "You need this."

I was afraid to ask what *this* referred to, but I was certain he was going to show me. His hand found my bare stomach again, but he didn't stop there. He continued down past the belt on my skirt and tucked the material between his hand and my legs. He rubbed me there and I reached back for his leg again. The cool air gained access to my legs as my skirt gathered in his hand. The hem raised up past my knees, past my thighs, past my soaked panties, and over my belt. He tucked it and pushed his fingers underneath the small elastic band of my underwear. I held my breath, my body trembling, my hands reassuring that my coat stayed down around me to shield me from the blank faces.

The moment he cupped my bare pussy, I inhaled deeply, forcibly, my head going back into his chest.

"Yes," he whispered. His fingers pushed into my lips and moved back and forth over my clit. If he continued doing that it'd be the fastest orgasm I'd ever had. But he knew this and stopped. I covered his hand with mine and tried directing him to continue, but he swiftly pulled my hand away with his free hand and bent it around my back between us.

"Don't do that again," he whispered.

He wanted complete control.

His fingers moved again. Arousal festered and threatened me. I moved my foot to the side, opening my legs for him. I needed to stop him soon. This was risky. Too risky. A little longer.

The subway train stopped and so did he, but his hand remained inside my panties. He held me there waiting as more than half of the people filed out the door and the train moved forward again. I glanced up at the sign. My stop was next, but his finger slipped inside me and his thumb rubbed my clit. I no longer cared who was around me, where I needed to be when the train stopped again, or how I was going to stop this stranger from finger fucking me.

"Listen to me carefully," he said quietly. "There are three more stops before this subway is retired for the evening. We will stay where we are until then."

My arousal heightened quickly but it was laced with panic and I tried turning toward him. He pinned me discreetly so that I couldn't.

"Your excitement for me comes because of the mystery. My excitement for you comes because I know you. I know what you need and I'm the man who can give it to you."

"I can't do this," I heard myself say.

"You can. I'll guide you." He pulled his hands away from me and I no longer felt him close to me. "If you truly do not want to continue, tell me now and I'll disappear forever."

I trembled harder. Did I want this to end so abruptly? I was just bitching in my mind about the humdrum life I was living. I was just telling myself I had wished for something exciting to happen for me. This wasn't quite what I had in mind, but it was here, rearing its sexual head and I had a choice to make.

The train stopped and the doors opened. I could hear myself breathing heavily. It was my stop. But I didn't move. My mind screamed for me to move, but my body froze where I stood. The doors closed and the train moved again.

"Good girl," he whispered. "You have pleased me." The warmth from his body radiated through me. His hand returned to my stomach. His tongue ran along the outside of my ear and his teeth nibbled the side before trailing down to my neck.

I closed my eyes when he cupped my pussy again, his fingers sliding inside me. My clit responded and added to the trembling I could not control.

My nipples ached for touch. I reached up and cupped them. My hardened nipples protruded through my bra and my blouse. They were hard against my palms and sensitive as I flicked them with my thumbs.

He pulled his hand from me, gripped my wrists, and pulled them to my side. "No. They are mine."

I forgot. He needs control. He pulled away, leaving me with my face against the wall, aching for his touch. I still sensed his body close to mine, but he withdrew from me. Why? Was he punishing me? I wanted his touch. I needed a release. Should I ask? Should I beg? I sucked my lower lip between my teeth and flicked it with the tip of my tongue. He was good and it made me crazy with arousal.

"I'm sorry," I whispered, slightly turning my head toward my shoulder I thought he was stood behind. The train stopped. The doors opened. He was still close but didn't say anything. He didn't touch me. He didn't move. I stared at the wall. The doors closed and the train moved one final time. Still nothing. I began to think I was imagining the warmth of his body and he had left me, but then he inhaled deeply. His hand slid around me once again and found my panties, then proceeded to delve deep into what was inside them. My arousal returned.

"The smell of your cunt intoxicates me," he growled, his lips brushing my ear. My arousal exploded.

He aggressively pushed his hand into my panties and his fingers into my pussy. They pushed deep inside me and almost completely withdrew before pushing back into me again. His other hand pressed against my back as leverage while he intrusively claimed every part of me. So many emotions were running rampant through me. I was scared to death, horny as hell, submissive to a stranger, and very aware that it was too late to stop this. I wanted to see him. I wanted to know who was dominating every fiber of my being. I wanted to know the man I was willing to give myself to without question.

But that was too late as well. The train stopped. The lights went out and we were alone. His fingers slowed. I could hear his breathing. It was ragged and labored. He let me go for the first time and I turned toward him. The only light came from a dim bulb on the outside tunnel wall and it was barely enough to see his silhouette.

"Who are you?" My mouth was dry. My body trembled uncontrollably, and I needed his hands on me but was afraid to tell him.

"Your savior." He wrapped his arm around my waist and pulled me into him, his mouth covering mine. He pushed his tongue past my lips and tasted me. I melted like butter in his arms until his hand pulled my blouse over my tits. He yanked my bra up and pushed me back until I bowed backward over his arm. He sucked my nipple into his mouth and bit down. Pain shot through me arrowing deep into my arousal and mixing them together deliciously. He held me there while his hand finger fucked me again. My arousal hit harder and an orgasm washed over me. I winced until his fingers stopped and he let me go.

I couldn't think. My brain was in a fog. He licked his fingers, taking my hand with his free hand and he led me to a seat in the corner. He unzipped his pants and pulled his cock free before sitting down in front of me. He directed me to my knees and slid his hand into my hair.

"Stroke it."

He was good at hitting my buttons. He had just pushed me to orgasm and I was feeling another one deep down inside me, merely by the words he said.

I reached out toward him, without hesitation, giddy with excitement that it was my turn to please him. My hand reached through the darkness and wrapped around it the moment my fingertips touched it. I stroked him and it felt so good. He was massive and thick, his veins bulging around it. I cupped his head and moved up and down the shaft. I licked my lips. I wanted to taste him. My eyes searched for his face, but it was futile. I couldn't see his face, only the shape of his head. What did he look like? I focused on his eyes but saw nothing but darkness. Moving my focus to the meat in my hand I wanted to please him. I wanted to make him happy. I wanted to submit to what he needed from me.

Stroking him felt empowering. I moved my hand along his heavy shaft pulling my hand with my arm in each direction. His head went back, and a moan escaped him. It was guttural and came from someplace deep in his throat. It fed my desire to please him. I sucked my bottom lip into my teeth, my body trembling with excitement. I leaned forward, my eyes glued to his exposed throat. My tongue ran across the tip of his dick and he immediately sprung his head forward.

"Yes," he growled. His fingers slid into the back of my hair and his grip tightened, my hair in his fist. "Suck me." He directed me forward and I easily complied. He was big but delicious. It filled my mouth easily. I wanted more. "Run your tongue up and down my shaft." His words were wavering, which meant I was doing a good job. I wanted to explore him further and I love that he told me what to do. He demanded my actions. And I complied, my tongue trying to move along his shaft as best as I could. He pressed my face down further and I knew I had more to engulf. But how? "Deeper," he grunted. When he pushed me further, I recognized the answer just before he demanded it. "Throat fuck it," he commanded. My throat was going to open whether I wanted it to or not. His head hit my gag reflex and I tried pulling away. His hand may as well have been a stone wall. I was there, not moving from my position, so I tried relaxing, squeezing my eyes closed. I had given blow jobs before but none of them were nearly this size. My ex-boyfriend was freaky, and we tried a lot of different things. It wasn't what I wanted, but I did it to try and please him. He had no response to what I did. I could have been doing everything right, or completely wrong. I had no way of knowing, so I left.

But this man, this stranger sitting before me knew just what to do and how to show me how I was doing. He directed me in ways I wished my ex would have done. Who would have known that I liked this so much? I opened my throat as he pushed me down further. I relaxed my muscles and caressed his thighs. Once it slid past the opening of my throat it moved easily and expanded my neck wide. He stopped and growled. He moved slowly back and forth and the friction of his dick moving along my esophagus made me want to swallow him. I wanted him in my throat, in my chest, in my stomach, in my pussy. I just wanted him to consume me. I bobbed my head up and down, slow at first then a little faster. My fingernails grazed along his balls and I felt them tighten against him. He let me go and I pulled myself off him, a deep breath of air forcing down into my lungs. I panted, I licked my lips, I tasted his pungent precum on my tongue and I wanted more. He laced my hair with his fingers again and pulled me down to his cock again. I eagerly opened my mouth and enjoyed the shape of it sliding against my tongue. Closing my lips around him I sucked him hard, bobbing my head up and down on his shaft.

"You are ready," he growled.

He stood up and pulled me to my feet, his mouth hungry for mine. He shared the taste of himself on my tongue. He moved his hands quickly to disrobe what he wanted bare. My skirt went up to my waist and my panties were pulled over to the side. He directed me to the seat where he had sat and turned me to face the window. I looked out but only saw a dimly lit tunnel wall with worn graffiti across it.

His hands went to my hips. I was dizzy with arousal. I felt his dick against my ass as he pushed the top of my back forward with his hand. He wanted me bent over in front of him, and I did. I grasped the sides of the seat and bent forward for him. My legs opened and I swallowed hard.

This was it. I should have stopped. But I couldn't. I was his no matter the consequence.

He pulled the bottom of my blouse up and caressed my back, his dick still pressed against me. He wasn't in any hurry, but he was making me crazy. I wanted to beg him to fuck me. I wanted to push him inside me and ride him like a rollercoaster until I orgasmed. Then I wanted to do it again. I wanted him to demand things from me I had never done before. I was ready. I was more willing than I ever thought I'd be.

"You are so fucking sexy." His words were low, deep and they hit me like a boulder. I would have done anything he asked. But he didn't ask. He just did what he wanted with me. And at that moment, he wanted to fuck me. He was ready.

He lined himself up and I felt him push against my vagina. He opened me slowly and stopped with each inch. I wanted to push back. I tried to push back, but he held me steady and did the work he wanted to do. He caressed my hips and my ass cheeks. He pushed a little deeper into me. He stopped and caressed me some more. I allowed the sensation to seep into me and felt it flow through me like hot water over cold skin. His hands gripped my hip bones and he pushed slowly inside me, opening me wide, stretching me further, and filling my pussy with his entire dick. It hurt, but it was addicting. He stopped and held me there, his arms sliding around my waist. His weight was on my back and his mouth was close to my face. He licked the back of my ear as he slowly withdrew himself from me. His weight lifted off me and he pushed back inside. He moved slowly, too slowly. I was screaming inside for release. I was desperate for him to fuck me hard and make me cum. I was aching so bad for more of him and I didn't care how he delivered himself to me.

I wanted to scream his name, but I didn't know who he was. I didn't know what he looked like, and I didn't know if I'd ever see him again. I needed to make this count. I needed to make him need me again. I'd ride this same subway next to this same wall for the rest of my life if it meant being with him again.

I gripped the seat harder and tried pushing back into him. The only thing I could do was open my legs for him further. And I did. He reached up underneath me and cupped my tits. He held them tight and fucked me steady. My breathing came harder, faster, drying my mouth but soaking my pussy.

"Oh, God," I whispered. My entire body quivered under his control. What else could he possibly do to me to make this any better? I was in complete ecstasy. When he pulled himself out and stood behind me, I was certain I was about to find out. His hands were still on my ass cheeks, caressing them, moving in circles around them, his fingers sliding up and down my crack. I felt him staring at me there, even though we couldn't see anything except silhouettes and the outside walls. He ran his finger down and pushed it inside me, my breath catching as he slid it out and up my anus. I knew what was next. It was something I had only done once, and it hurt like hell. He was going to fuck my ass.

A new wave of fear spread through me. This man behind me was at least twice the size of my ex-boyfriend and I remember the pain well. When he stepped forward and I felt the head of his dick touch me there I jumped and moved forward a bit.

"I don't know if I...."

He stopped me by sliding his hand over my mouth. He pulled me upright and kissed my neck, his teeth grazing my skin.

"Don't speak. Don't say no. Don't," he whispered. His hand was still over my mouth as his other hand cupped my tit. He rolled my nipple between his fingers and electricity struck me down to my cunt. His hand moved slightly over my mouth so he could push two fingers in over my tongue. He slid them in and out as he played with my nipple, pinching it and twirling it until it was raw and sensitive. "Who do you belong to," he growled close to my ear. His words made me squirm with enthusiasm.

"You," I whispered.

"Yes. I know now where to find you and I will again. This isn't our first encounter, my pet. I will find you here again when I need to. When you need me to."

I nodded and lowered myself to the seat again. I could barely breathe, but each breath was heavy and deep. I could barely feel but every fiber of my being was electric and ready to explode. I could barely move but I was willing to move any way he wanted me to. I opened my legs and waited with anticipation.

"Good girl." His hands caressed my ass and moved along my pussy. He inserted his fingers again, finger fucking me slowly before pulling them out and sliding them across my anus. The moment his dick touched me there I flinched. But he stopped. He was good. He was slow. Sympathetic to my needs and my desires. The more pressure he gave the more heat I felt.

He pushed until my hole opened slightly, fighting its intrusion but exciting the hell out of everything beyond it. His hands moved in wide circles over my cheeks, slowly only to push himself a little deeper. I thought my brain would explode. The pain and the pleasure he fed me was so intense I honestly felt I was going crazy. I inhaled sharply and exhaled with a shaky breath. I gripped the seat so hard I thought it would break in my hands. I stiffened every muscle in my body until I felt they would cramp into position. He pushed deeper and stopped for a moment. He rocked back and forth, and something deep inside me welled up and began to surround me.

"No, no, no," he whispered, stopping his movement, but caressing with his hands. "Not yet, my pet. We have all night and I want this to last." He stroked my body as the pressure inside me slowly dissipated. I tried to swallow but my tongue was dry. I inhaled slowly and tried to focus but the darkness kept that from me as well.

When he began to move again, I concentrated on his body behind me. I imagined the way he moved, and what he saw, and the position of his back as he rocked back and forth. I felt that pressure deep inside again but worked on controlling it and the pace that it consumed me. He pushed deeper and I deliciously invited the pain in, mentally swirling it with the heated desire radiating from every part of me. I opened my legs further, as he slowly began fucking my asshole. His hands found my tits and he lightly caressed them as they swayed back and forth over his palms. He knew how to intensify my desires, he knew how to control what I wanted, he knew how to manipulate what I needed to mold it to his desires. He knew me deeper than I knew myself and he was exactly what I needed in my life. To control my inner desires, to be controlled by a dominant man that knew how to touch those desires.

I pushed back into him, my head moving back. My hair fell over my bareback and he scooped it up to hold me there. His fist tight around my hair, he pulled me back into him and fucked me harder.

"You're my whore, now," he growled. "Say it."

I let out a guttural groan from my tightened throat. It was all I could manage.

He yanked my head back a little harder and stopped fucking me. "Say it," he demanded.

"I'm…yours," I grunted.

"You're my whore." He began fucking me again as if it were my reward for complying with his demands.

"Yes." I tried nodding but it wasn't possible.

"You're going to be my whore whenever I choose you to be." His pace got a little faster.

"Yes." My voice trembled.

"I will fuck you when I see fit, but you will never know when that will be. I will fuck you where I want, but you'll never know when I'll be there."

I inhaled a shaky breath as the pressure built inside me. He fucked me faster, harder, his groin slamming into me with each thrust.

"This. Will. Be. Your. Wake up. Call." He grabbed my hips and slammed into me one more time before filling me up with everything he had. His yell echoed off the walls. His hands gripped me hard and my muscles tightened like a vice around his dick. I came so hard I stopped breathing and froze. My legs quaked underneath me. He withdrew his dick from my ass, and I collapsed into the seat, breathing hard, shivering from my head to my feet and naked except for my skirt still around my waist and my panties still off to the side. They were soaked.

He gathered me into his arms and scooped me up onto his lap. His hand caressed my hair until I calmed myself down and my breathing became somewhat normal again.

"Who are you," I whispered, looking up at him. Although my eyes had adjusted a little more in the darkened subway car, I still strained to see the whites of his eyes, unsuccessfully, however.

"I'm your savior, as I said before. You will no longer go through your days wondering why you're doing what you're doing, and why you feel stuck in a life you do not desire. The anticipation of seeing me or feeling me behind you again will change your entire existence."

"Just like that? You won't tell me who you are? I just gave myself to you."

"You did. You're a rare breed, my pet. You have given me as much as I have given you. As much as you are my whore, I am your savior. I am a new outlook on each day you wake up. I am an excitement you will look forward to each time you come onto this subway. Or perhaps in a café you frequent, or the fitting room at Macy's. How long have I been watching you?"

My heart skipped a beat. I had put myself into a bad situation, fucking a stranger, allowing him access to parts of me I wasn't even aware existed. And now that he has gotten in, I didn't think I was going to get him out again. He was right. He just changed my life. The anticipation of him lurking around each corner I rounded was going to keep my pussy wet and my stomach tightly knotted. How would I know when I passed him on the street? How would I know if he drove the next Uber I climbed into? How would I react if he was my next client at work and I had to work with him on a daily basis? How would I know? How would I keep my sanity?

"Stand up." He lifted me off him and I stood on my weak legs, still half-naked but worried this was the end of our time together. He knelt in front of me and ran his hands up my legs. My arousal returned. He caressed me between my legs, and I opened for him further. He tasted us on his fingers, his breath catching as he did.

His forehead rested against my stomach and held onto my hips. It was the first vulnerable moment I witnessed with him. It gave me strength and a need to take care of him. I stroked his hair and decided it was dark, perhaps black. And his eyes, they were blue, icy, deep. He hooked my underwear in his hand and repositioned them where they belonged before pulling my skirt back down into place. Rising to his feet, he towered over me at least a foot and assisted me with my blouse. He handed my bra back and I felt around and found my bag, pushing my bra inside it. Turning around, I let him slide my coat back onto my arms. He buttoned it and held on for a few moments more.

Not another word was spoken, but everything each of us needed surrounded us at that moment. He walked to the doors and pulled them apart, waiting for me, to assist me to the concrete platform just outside the car. I stepped out but kept my head down. There may have been enough light to see him, but at that moment I didn't want that. I merely waited for him to walk with me, but he did not.

"Until we meet again, my pet." He kissed my palm and walked the opposite way until he was out of sight from me.

Would I ever see him again? Would there be a next time? I was already aching for him. He was still very much around me, in my head, in my body. The evidence was there, and I didn't want to wash it away. My soaked underwear, uncomfortable against my swollen pussy was evidence. My ass sore from his cock. My mind no longer bored and defeated. He changed that just like he said he would.

The next morning, I went through my same routine but looked for him around every corner I rounded. I looked into every man's eyes, wondering if they were the ones I searched for that night in the subway car. Each man could have been him. Each man I walked by, each guy I caught glancing my way, any of them could have been him. What if I already knew him? A co-worker? My boss? The mail carrier? I was going crazy not knowing.

That night when I got back to my apartment, I dropped everything and lay on the couch. My body was on fire for his touch. I slid my hand into my pants and fingered myself, my mind drowned in thoughts of him. An orgasm hit me hard before I showered and went to bed. Maybe the next day would be different.

Every day was much like that day. Every day became a new hope, full of anticipation on the what if. What if that day was the next time I encountered him? What if it was in the subway again? What if it was a café bathroom? What about a stock room at the local grocery store? He changed me. And I was grateful for that.

A week and a half went by with no signs of him. I was beginning to think it was a dream. He wasn't even real. Until the day he was. I stood next to the same wall, similar faces around me. Every nudge of an elbow heightened my senses. Every brush of a body aroused me. When his presence was behind me and I felt the warmth of his body again I began to tremble much like the first time. His body moved in close and his hand slid around my waist. My breath stuck in my throat like glue. I lowered my head and inhaled a shaky breath.

"Yes," he whispered. "We meet again, my pet."

We stood there for the entire ride, very close, his hand roaming my body under my coat as the crowd thinned from the car with every stop. When the train made its final destination, and the lights went out he turned me toward him. His mouth covered mine and his tongue claimed what it wanted. We were both hungry for each other, but he was urgent, non-sensitive, non-caring. I didn't mind. He was with me.

He sucked my chin into his mouth and traveled down my neck, biting at my skin and groping me with a hunger I hadn't witnessed before. He ripped my dress open from the front and yanked my bra up. He grabbed my arms and leaned down as if he needed to milk me. He sucked my tit into his mouth and devoured it. I stared down at him, eyes wide, trying to focus, trying to see any glimpse of him I could in the dim bulb from outside the subway car. He kneaded my tits with his hands as he licked and bit at my nipples before sliding his hand down my stomach and under my dress. He quickly found my panties and yanked them down urgently. I stepped out of them, breathless and trembling. Without warning he reached up between my legs and pushed his fingers inside me, finger fucking me fast and furiously. I wanted to tell him to slow down. I wanted to ask him why he was so desperate. I wanted to pleasure him like I did the first time, but he wasn't having it.

He pushed his fingers inside me over and over again until my pussy began to hurt. Where was his sexy dominance? Where was his need to control and take his time? I was confused and I didn't want to be there, but I didn't try to stop him. He stood up and I could hear him sucking on his fingers before he leaned into me and kissed me hard. I tasted what he did on his tongue and it surged through me. He spun me around and shoved my upper body forward. I flopped over, my hands barely catching the seat in front of me. I held the metal bar with one hand and the corner of the seat with my other. He didn't allow me to straighten up. He was there for one thing and that scared the hell out of me. I heard the jingle of his belt before he jerked my dress up over my hips. He stroked my pussy and ran it along my asshole before penetrating it.

Oh God! He was going straight for my ass!

I squeezed my eyes closed and braced for the pain. He pushed into me. All. The. Way. No hesitation, no taking his time. He pushed into me and held me there until I stretched and relaxed around his dick. Then he began to move. He grunted with every thrust into my ass and the pain didn't have enough pleasure to mix with.

I clenched my teeth tightly and held my breath, trying to put my mind someplace else until he was satisfied, but it took forever. Over an hour he fiercely fucked me without recourse. I reached down between my legs to help things along, expecting him to yank my hand away but he didn't. I sliced my fingers through the folds of my pussy and teased my swollen clit trying to get some satisfaction from this heinous act and eventually, arousal sparked. As he slammed into me repeatedly, I worked at my sensitive clit and expanded my arousal, eventually pushing back into him hoping for a better response. He never changed his rhythm or his demeanor, but I did cum. In the few moments before I did, I welcomed his intrusion and begged him to fuck my ass harder. Once I was finished, he continued for another fifteen minutes, at least. He was troubled by something and he needed release, not just from his body but from whatever was messing with his mind. I was his vessel, and I thought I was okay with that. My knees wanted to buckle, and my back wanted to break. How long could I withstand this treatment? I had to tell him to stop.

He gripped my hips harder, pushing into me deeper, grunting a little louder. This gave me the strength to hold out just a little longer. He blew his load, grunting from someplace deep inside him. It sliced through me like a knife, like I could feel what he was going through. His cock pulsated inside me while he worked to calm his body and regulate his breathing. He pulled out and I stood up, my legs weak from supporting him for so long. I attempted to touch him, but he turned away and pulled his pants up, his buckle clinking together.

"Are you...okay?" I asked softly.

He didn't respond. I pulled my bra down and attempted to fix my dress, but it was too damaged, so I buttoned my coat closed and stood before him watching his outline. He turned back to me and held my face in his hands for a moment.

"Some days will be exactly like this. It's what I needed."

He walked to the doors and pulled them open before disappearing around the corner. I fought back tears as I searched for my underwear and clenched my coat over my chest. I had no reason to cry. I was shaking, yes, but only because it was so abrupt and callous, yet I felt like I gave him exactly what he needed.

Days fed into weeks and my masturbation became more frequent. This man had left me in a state I couldn't control and every chance I had I was touching myself. I walked into a coffee shop to grab a cup to go, but more so to borrow their bathroom for some privacy. Walking into a stall, I locked myself inside and waited for two others to leave. Once it was quiet, I removed my bra from underneath my thin blouse and shoved it into my bag. Sliding my hand underneath my skirt I moved slowly fingering my clit and imagining his hands on my body and his cock in my ass. I made small circles around my hardened nipple feeling my arousal spread quickly. His aggressions were justified, and I felt I helped him cope with whatever demons he was dealing with. I didn't have to ask. I just needed to be. For him.

I closed my eyes and listened to my breathing as it got heavier. I looked down at my thumb as I mimicked what he did the first night we were together, and a folded piece of paper laid on the floor between my feet. I froze and listened intently. I was still alone, wasn't I?

I turned my head to read the upside-down writing and gasped at the words.

"Perhaps it's time to go beyond the subway. Regency on Broadway. Room 415. This evening."

A familiar tremble returned deep inside my stomach as I picked up the note and read it again. My other hand opened the stall door slowly as I peeked around the room. There was no one there.

"What the hell?" What was I feeling? Panic? Excitement? Fear? My mouth went dry.

I left the bathroom with the note clutched in my hand and a deep arousal in my belly. Standing before the barista I couldn't understand why the young man was grinning so much until I looked down. I never put my bra back on and the thought of finally meeting the mystery man had me so horny my nipples were telling the world.

"Uh," I raised my arm to cover them, but then lowered it again. I was tired of being invisible. It was freeing to know I was the reason for this kid's grin and potential erection behind the counter, even though it did take hard nips to make it happen. I smirked and straightened my posture before I ordered a chai latte with extra cream, three m's, and a smile.

The rest of my day I spent with pins and needles and my underwear soaked between my legs. I don't know how I made it through work, but I did, and the evening was upon me. I had fought with myself all day on whether I should go to this hotel room with this man. I didn't know him even though I have had his semen inside me. But he would have killed me by now if that was his thing. No. This was much more than that. He needed me as much as I needed him. It was fucked up, but it was my fuck up.

Maybe he wanted to take our relationship further. No matter how much I questioned it, I was not passing this opportunity up. I was finally going to see him, to know who this man was. Was I right to decide he had black hair and piercing blue eyes?

After I went home and showered for an hour, I carefully selected a simple black dress over a black lace bra and panty, something classy for him to see me in. The entire time I prepared myself for him I felt excitement. But my stomach felt sick once I stood in front of the door at the Regency Hotel. I opened it and walked inside as I tried to regulate my breathing. I was greeted with friendly smiles and beautiful décor as I walked through the lobby.

"Excuse me, miss?" The attendant at the desk smiled when I looked at her. "Can I help you?"

"I'm meeting someone." I didn't want to answer any questions. I didn't know who I was meeting, and at that moment I felt cheap, like a hooker meeting a client.

"Yes, miss. I was directed to give you this." The attendant held a key card toward me and smiled. "You'll be in room 415."

I scrunched my eyebrows down and hesitatingly took it from her. "That's right, but...how did you know I...." I looked around but saw nothing peculiar.

"It's okay, miss. You can go up. He has been expecting you."

I nodded slightly, still defensive, but I forced a smile and made my way up to room 415.

I shook my arms as I stared at the gold numbers on the door and breathed deep a few times before sliding the card across the lock. Opening the door slightly I peeked inside but he didn't appear to be there yet. The door closed behind me as I looked around the room. It would give me a little time to get used to being there. The room was beautiful, clean, with a bottle of wine waiting on the desk next to a white box and a note.

I walked to the desk and read the note.

Enjoy. Wine to relax with. A gift for you as well.

I opened the box, and it was a dress very similar to the one he ripped off me. *He does have a heart after all,* I smiled. In the middle of the dress was another small box with another note.

Wear this for me now and await my arrival.

I was giddy with excitement as I opened the box and pulled out a black silk blindfold.

"Shit." My insides turned to mush.

I opened the wine and filled the glass halfway, chugging half of it. I stared at the blindfold as the sweet taste spread across my tongue. It warmed my face quickly and lowered my inhibitions. I pulled the blindfold from the box and slid it through my fingers. It was soft, silky, teasing me, and demanding me to wear it. I didn't at first, but then I felt guilty. He wanted me to. I sat on the bed and placed it over my eyes, tying it loosely at the back. I nodded in approval. It wasn't so bad. Intriguing. Sexy. A smidge of light peeked from underneath it and if I tilted my head the right way, I could see a bit of my surroundings.

I sat there only a few minutes when I heard the door open quietly. My breath caught and I wanted to be sure it was him, but I didn't move my head. What did I call him? How would I be able to tell? I chuckled nervously to myself and listened intently. The door clicked closed and the moments grew longer. The silence was deafening. I jumped when I felt a hand on my face raising my head. It slid down to my chest and copped a feel, squeezing slightly before disappearing into the silence again. I turned my head to the side desperate for something, a sound, a word, something.

"Take off your bra and whatever else you have underneath."

I trembled at the familiar tone of his voice, making it a little harder for me to climb off the bed. I reached underneath my dress and removed my panties stepping out of them when I felt them fall down my legs. I pulled the straps of my bra out of my dress and fed my arms out of them, pulling it from underneath and discarding it at my feet. I could see them through the small opening at the bottom of my blindfold.

I didn't know what to do with my hands. I didn't know if I should get back on the bed or stay where I was. I didn't know if he was in front of me with his eyes on me or where he was. The blindfold over my eyes tightened quickly and I sucked in a little air, reaching up and barely touching it. The opening was gone, and I was in complete darkness again, just how he liked it.

"Drink," he said softly.

I felt the glass on my lower lip and opened my mouth until the sweetness filled my mouth. The moment I swallowed it, his mouth was on mine and his tongue was lapping up the taste. It threw me into overdrive without hesitation.

"Why are we here?" I asked, a quiver in my voice.

"You know the answer, my pet."

"I mean, I thought this was my chance to finally see you."

Silence filled the spaces around me. I reached up and slid my fingers along the mask. I wanted to pull it down. What would he do? Would he stop seeing me? The thought was horrifying.

His hands tightened around my wrists and they were lowered to my side. "Keep it," he whispered close to my ear. Chills. I nodded slightly. "Good girl."

He was close to me. His heat warmed me. I was lifted off the floor and the next thing I felt was the bed underneath me. I reached my arms out to either side. He had me in the middle, I didn't feel the mattress move with the weight of his body. I didn't hear the tone of his deep voice. I didn't smell his scent close to me. I moved my head to the side hearing only the silence around me once again.

"You look beautiful lying there in that dress."

My lower lip quivered. He was watching me. His voice came from the foot of the bed. "I want to see you." I shouldn't have requested again, but I did. My words dissipated into the room.

My legs were pushed open and I felt the air surround my pussy immediately. I felt his eyes there, his hands on my legs, the weight of him on the bottom of the bed. Hands slid slowly up my legs and brought the bottom of my dress with them as he moved to my hips. Arousal threatened my insides as a tickle cascaded over my mound. Warmth. Another tickle. More warmth. Was he breathing on it? I spread further.

"So fucking beautiful."

My lips were parted open and something slid inside me. His fingers? Two hands reached up and grabbed each of my arms holding me tight, and I gasped. He had his mouth on me, his tongue sliding inside my folds and flicking over my clit. I opened my legs as far as they could go, and my head went back in ecstasy. I moved my hips back and forth moaning at the sensation he pushed into me. His hands tightened around my arms as he tasted me and fucked me with his tongue bringing me to a delicious orgasm.

He moved on the bed, to the side of me but he was no longer touching me.

"You are an incredible woman. I'm very fortunate to have found you." His voice trailed away telling me he had his back to me. "What you have given me…."

"Are you breaking up with me?" I sat up quickly and reached my hand toward him.

"No," he chuckled. "Is this a relationship?"

"It's something, isn't it? You flood my brain daily. I dream about you every night."

"Hush, my pet. I'm not leaving you. I'm giving you an option."

"An option?"

"You have an image of me," he said, his deep tone surrounding me.

"Yes." I was a little too excited with my response but perhaps? Was he going to let me see him?

"Having the ability to create an image in your mind is why a book is better than the movie."

"I agree but, sometimes the reality of things is better than one could ever imagine."

"Sometimes. Other times not so much." He took my hand and sandwiched it between his. "What we have is beyond names and faces. You have given me so much without asking why. You have touched me deeper than anyone in my life. For this, I will leave it to you. You have one minute to decide. You can remove your mask and see me, or you can choose to keep it where it is. If you choose to keep it on, this will be our *relationship*. If you want to see me, things will change. They will never be as they are now."

I sat up and curled my legs toward me. Was he honestly giving me the option? I reached up and pinched the material with my fingers but stopped before I pulled it down. Was I ready to see him and shatter the image I had of him? It honestly didn't matter what he looked like. A drop-dead gorgeous narcissist or an average joe with sadistic tendencies. We both satisfied each other, and it no longer mattered what he looked like.

I leaned back and settled down onto the pillow, clasping my hands together across my stomach until the minute had passed.

His weight shifted on the bed until he was lying next to me, his arm draped over me, his head on my chest. I wrapped my arms around him and just held on.

"I like this," he said, his finger sliding along the swells of my breasts. "It makes me feel wholesome and cherished."

It was an odd thing for a dominant man to say next to a half-naked woman with a blindfold on, but I didn't question it. He had his reasons. I was just happy to satisfy him, no matter what he needed.

~CHAPTER 2~

Wife Gets Gangbanged During A House Break-In

A Gangbang is Needed — Sex with her husband has become a normal and quite typical half-hour. Same position, same thoughts, same fantasy. When their house is broken into during one of their sessions, three men creep through only expecting to rob them. They never expected to encounter the couple having sex. They watch until the husband notices them. He tries to protect his wife, but they have other plans. It's time to show this guy how to treat his wife properly.

~HER~

The position I slept in had cradled my body long enough. Keeping my eyes closed, I pushed myself over to my other side and curled up into Ronald, stealing his body heat and trying to wish myself back into my dream. I rarely remembered my dreams, but when I did, I hung onto them for as long as I could. They were almost always erotic and seductive, and I used them as my fantasies during our sexy time, as Ronald liked to call it.

I squeezed my eyes tighter and imagined myself back in the dream.

I couldn't see much with the blinding lights all around me, the heat from them producing sweat that trickled down the middle of my naked back. It was as if I was sitting on a stage and the hot lights were keeping the audience from my vision. Was I in a play? Was it something rehearsed or was it improv? There was no noise, no depth to the room I was in. I could have been alone, but somehow, I knew I wasn't.

A hand was placed on my shoulder. It moved, caressing me and massaging my neck. Two fingers under my chin lifted my head toward the blinding lights and all I could do was squint. A pair of lips on the side of my neck kissed me there, his tongue occasionally licking my skin. Another pair of hands coasted along the curves of my hips, up and down, slowly, seductively, exquisitely.

I didn't know these men who had conjured around me, but I loved the awakening I was receiving from their touch. I held onto a metal bar above my head a little tighter. Not knowing where they were going to touch me next was the biggest turn-on I had ever experienced, but it wasn't an experience, was it? It was only a dream. A gorgeous, luscious, opulent dream that I didn't want to end.

My legs were pushed open and a man crawled toward me, his head appearing between them. I could only see the back of his head, so I locked my eyes onto his luscious black curls, my mouth falling open. My heart pounded against the inside of my chest. Excitement trembled through me. The lights dimmed and my eyes adjusted to several beautiful men all naked and all horny for me. The man between my legs lifted his head slightly, and I locked my eyes on his face. He was dark and so sexy. His hands glided up my thighs, his dark chocolate hands contrasting against my pale skin. His tongue slithered out of his mouth and licked the inside of my thigh, achingly close to my sweet spot. I swallowed hard, my heavy breathing drying my mouth out. Hands slithered up and down my arms before moving to my chest. They picked my tits up and pressed them together before a blond-haired man blocked my view and lapped at my nipples. The tongue on my thigh that was dangerously close to my pussy, threatening to tease me there no longer threatened. The blond had moved just in time for me to witness the tip of the black man's tongue doing exactly what it threatened to do. It flicked my clit lightly, his dark eyes looking up at me and seizing my complete attention.

My pussy ached for satisfaction. It ached for a cock to fuck. It screamed out for a man to take me and dominate me.

His tongue flicked faster, harder, his hands moving back and forth across my thighs. He settled his lips around my pussy, and he began to hum. The deep tone of his voice sent volts of electricity through me before his tongue pushed into me. I grabbed the sides of the bench I sat on and gripped it hard.

A pair of hands slid down from my shoulders from someone standing behind me, the naked bulge of his cock pressing against my back. It moved up and down against me, slowly at first. As he picked up his speed, I knew he was getting off on me. I offered myself to him, *but the man between my legs wouldn't share just yet. He continued licking me until arousal swarmed around me and threatened to make me cum.*

I moved against the man behind me, his breathing more rugged than before. He was close. Another man stood idly by and stroked himself as he watched. I pressed back harder, looked down at the hands on my thighs, and left my body. I floated up into the air and looked down at four naked gods getting off on getting me off. I tried pushing myself back down to my body but the harder I tried the higher I floated. I could still see the tongue lapping at my pussy, and the cock sliding furiously up and down my back, his head falling back before he shot a load up my back. I floated higher, screaming for them to stop before I came. I wanted to feel it. I needed to feel it. I ached for it but could no longer have it.

"No!" I screamed. "Wait! Don't do it!" I desperately grabbed at the air around me and tried to swim back down to them. It was working, but I had to flail my arms hard and fast to get there. Sweat poured off me but I did manage to get close enough to settle back into my body.

The man between my legs was still watching my face and the moment I looked into his eyes a pair of hands grabbed my arms and pushed me away again.

"No!" I screamed.

"Victoria," a voice whispered.

The lights around me brightened again, blinding me, and everything stopped. I reached out into the bright light, begging for them to return. The lights died and I felt nothing but the coldness of the air around me.

"Victoria. Wake up."

My eyes flew open and I tried looking around the dark room. Where did the lights go? Where did my lovers go? "No," I mumbled. "Come back. I wasn't finished."

"Are you okay? Wake up."

"What? Where am I?"

"You're in bed. It's two in the morning. You must have been having quite a nightmare."

My heart sank. Nope. It wasn't a nightmare.

"You kept begging for someone to help you. Are you okay?"

"I'm fine." My tone was sleepy and slurred. "I don't remember it."

It was easier to lie than to tell him about it. He was never much for fantasy when it came to sex.

I snuggled into him hoping to get a little reward for the arousal that didn't go away when the dream faded. He merely kissed my shoulder and rolled the other way leaving me frustrated and horny. It wasn't our normal sexy time.

Ronald liked everything to be structured and in place, including time for sex. It got a little boring at times, but he was massive in all the right areas which made it good when we did fuck.

A soft snoring sound came from his side of the bed but no matter how hard I tried I couldn't get back to sleep. I imagined the hands on me again, the tongue inside me, the hard cock on my back, but nothing worked. I stared at the clock on the bedside table and the red numbers told me I still had three hours of lying there in my current state.

I rolled onto my stomach and pushed my hand underneath me, my fingers working into my panties. I positioned the tip of my finger between my lips so that when I moved it tingles would begin to form there and spread through me. Careful not to move the bed too much, I moved my finger back and forth imagining the dream I was dragged from. It wasn't long before a wave of pleasure wafted through me and the challenge was not to move until I was satiated. Well, as satiated as I could be. I sighed and enjoyed pulses that came from the muscles between my legs, allowing the numbing sensation of sleep to waft over me.

The alarm dragged me from my sleep and moments later Ronald's arm wrapped around me. It was his way of telling me he wanted sex.

The mornings he wanted a little were like this. He'd rub my stomach with his hands while he spooned me from behind. I'd glide my fingers along his arm until his cock pushed into my backside, then he'd roll me onto my back so he could climb on top, push my legs apart and *tease* me until he entered me and moved back and forth at his pace. His kisses got me more than his so-called teasing, but I took what I could get. He was very vanilla, but he was a damn good kisser. What he did with his tongue drove me crazy. I just wished he'd use his tongue in other places besides my mouth.

And it's not like I haven't tried different things or suggested changing it up. The way he'd look at me when I mentioned doing it in a public bathroom or even in the living room over the end of the sofa, you'd think I suggested something illegal like making him watch a bunch of big muscular men have their way with me. I smiled slightly at the thought, my dream flooding back to me. I closed my eyes and played it back in my head as Ronald continued moving back and forth inside me.

The contrast of that man's skin against mine, the feel of his tongue lapping at my pussy, the other men surrounding me all waiting their turn aroused me. I grabbed Ronald's ass and pulled him into me with each thrust, but it didn't change the pace or seem to turn him on any different than what I was used to. He pulled himself back and looked at me quizzically before smiling and burying his head back into the crook of my neck.

"Fuck me, Ronnie."

After a very nice orgasm, I stayed in bed for as long as I could before having to rush about to get ready for my day. I had a big meeting with some incredible artists for a new gallery show I have been working on for next month and I was feeling good about it. It was our semi-annual show, and a lot of the proceeds would help my gallery through several months until I booked the next one.

Ronald sat at the table and dove into his half of a grapefruit. "So, are you ready for your meeting today?"

"I think so." I guzzled half a glass of water and popped a handful of vitamins into my mouth washing them down with the last of it before grabbing a banana and heading back into the bedroom to select my attire.

"Are you nervous? I know the last meeting you had didn't go very well."

"No, thanks to the client."

"Clients always get what they want. You know that. It's just business, Victoria."

I don't know why he insisted on calling me by my proper name. Vicky was fine. Hell, I was even okay with Vic. Victoria made me sound like I was stuck up and bitchy. I didn't like that.

"I know," I said, throwing the banana peel away and devouring the fruit in only a few bites. "And they did, remember? That doesn't mean I have to like it." I turned the shower on and let the cold water run on my hand until it got warmer. Ronald walked in behind me and stripped down, stealing the shower before I could even protest.

"You're very good at your job. Don't let anyone tell you differently."

I pulled my top off and wiggled out of my panties before joining him. "Hand me your soap. I'll wash your back." I hoped it was enough.

"What are you doing?"

"Taking a shower with my husband." I kissed his nose and held my hand out. "Soap?"

"This shower is too small for the both of us. You know that."

"So, get closer," I smirked.

"Victoria. I have to get to the office. I have big deadlines."

I exhaled the air from my lungs and climbed back out. "You don't have to schedule *everything,* ya know."

"I'm a scheduler. You knew that when you married me," he said poking his head out and smiling. "Nice bum, by the way."

I smiled back until he disappeared behind the curtain. "You didn't even look at it," I mumbled leaving the bathroom with a pout. I sauntered into the bedroom and stopped in front of the full-length mirror on the wall. I looked at myself and analyzed my features. My breasts were pretty good in size. Thirty-four D was good, healthy. Right? My waist was still small, and I worked out a few times a week, so my stomach was flat. I turned and looked at my bum and ran my hand along my curves. It was still firm and tight. "Hmm." I turned back around and slid my hands up my stomach to my breasts, cupping them and pushing them together.

"What are you doing?" Ronald stood in the doorway with a towel around him.

"Am I attractive?" I stared at my face and cocked my head.

"What are you talking about? Of course, you are. I wouldn't be with an ugly woman." He went to his dresser and opened the second drawer.

"So, if I aged and wasn't so in shape, you'd leave me?" I wasn't sure where I was going with this. I wasn't insecure in the slightest.

"I don't define ugly like that. Where is this coming from?" Never skipping a step from his morning routine, he only glanced over at me a couple of times.

"I don't know. I guess I'm getting a little bored with our daily routine. Aren't you?"

"What would you like to do? We could take a small vacation, maybe fly to Italy for the weekend. Or, I can get the sailboat and we can go sailing to the Keys."

"Maybe." I sighed and left him in the room. It wasn't what I was referring to, and I knew he'd never get it.

Before long, he was kissing me goodbye and walking out the door. "We will talk about it more this evening over dinner."

I tried staying busy as my stomach wreaked havoc on my nerves. I positioned and repositioned some of the artwork in the gallery, my eyes constantly looking up at the clock on the wall. When my new clients arrived the door chime sounded and I exhaled quickly. I plastered a smile on my face and went around the corner toward the door. My clients were all men and all very good-looking. I chuckled a little when my first thought was my dream from the night before. Imagining their hands on me sort of calmed my nerves as they introduced themselves. It was sort of similar to when you have stage fright, and you imagine the audience naked.

"It's good to meet you," I said, my smile more genuine than the one I started with. "We can sit here and begin our meeting." I motioned them toward a large round table in the corner of the gallery. "Would you like anything? Coffee? Tea? Water?"

I caught one of them descending their eyes down my body. I managed to look away before they noticed. "No. Thank you," he said sitting across from me.

"Aaron, right?" I asked, staring back at him.

"Yes."

Aaron had big blue eyes, icy and mesmerizing to look into. He was smooth with his words and charismatic with his actions. He didn't look much like an artist, but in my career, you didn't mention that. Whether you were good or not was in the eye of the beholder. Anyone could be an artist whether you looked like a calendar fireman or a jock fresh out of college, or if you look more like Stahlin. My eyes shifted to him.

Stahlin was more the artistic type, his long black hair thrown back in a messy pony. You could tell by looking at him that he was gay with a hint of bisexuality. Watching him with the other three I would have put money on the fact they weren't just comrades by art. I had an inkling he was a little more friendly with a couple of them from time to time. He was sexy, deep, and mysterious.

Rufus was the straight-laced one. He was the manager of the bunch and had a computer in his hands more than a paintbrush or a coal pencil or lump of clay. Coordinator and scheduler, he knew his shit and how to try and manipulate things to go his way. I was ready to deal.

Then there was Malcolm. He was beautiful and a challenge for me. It was rather ironic that I was married to Ronald, the whitest and most straight-laced man I had ever met because African American men always did it for me. And this man in front of me was hopefully gay. His dark skin glowed and his black eyes pierced through me. I wanted nothing more than to jump on the front of him and ride him like a bull in a rodeo.

I cleared my throat and forced my focus on Rufus through most of the meeting, all the while noticing how wet I was getting between my legs. Why did I have to dream about a gang of men touching me just before I sat in the middle of a gang of men? It wasn't fair.

The moment I booked them and they left the gallery I went up the stairs to my office and closed my door. I leaned against it and closed my eyes, inhaling deeply. *Jesus Christ that was hard,* I thought. As if it had a mind of its own, my hand moved across my thigh and rubbed myself through my pants. It ignited something deep inside me.

The wall facing the gallery was all glass, so I tucked myself into the opposite corner almost out of sight and leaned back in my chair. Cupping my breasts with both hands I felt my nipples harden and it thrilled me to rub my thumbs over them. I closed my eyes and slid my hand down my stomach and into my pants. With one hand on my tit and the other rubbing my pussy, it didn't take long to develop a rhythm with my fingers as arousal bled through me. My dream replayed in my head but this time with the faces of Malcolm, Aaron, Stahlin, and Rufus.

Looking down between my legs, Malcolm looked up at me as he devoured me with his luscious mouth. His tongue darted inside me, pushing my lips open. I hummed as deep as I could, my fingers pushing into my cunt.

I picked up my foot and found a place for it on the corner of my desk as I fingered myself faster and worked myself into a heated frenzy that sent waves crashing over me. I clutched the arm of my chair until it subsided, enjoying pulses between my legs. When I opened my eyes, I caught a glimpse of someone in the gallery. I stood up and adjusted myself before turning toward the hopeful customer. But it wasn't a customer at all. Malcolm was standing in the middle of the gallery looking up at me. His portfolio was still on the table where we sat. I should have been mortified, but something inside me caught fire again at the idea that he watched me pleasure myself.

I didn't move. He slowly walked to the table, blindly scooped up his portfolio, and left, all the while keeping his eyes glued to mine.

"Oh my God," I shuddered as the door closed behind him.

~HIM~

I was frozen where I stood in the middle of the Gallery. I never dreamt in a million years I would look up and see her pleasuring herself and satisfying her carnal needs. I should have been the one up there taking care of that for her. My cock hardened when she looked at me and didn't move. She wasn't upset or embarrassed. I think she liked me watching her. I wondered if she wanted more. I kept my eyes on her as I located My Portfolio I had left behind. Should I go to her? Should I satisfy her the way she should be satisfied? She was an angel from heaven, and she needed to be saved.

~HER~

He stuck with me, in my head the rest of the day and when I had gotten home Ronald was already there and already immersed in whatever it was he was doing on his computer.

"You're home early," I said, setting my bag on the table.

"Actually, you're home late." He nodded toward the clock before going back to his computer.

"Ah, so I am." I walked up behind him and slid my hands around his neck, kissing the side of his face. "How was your day?"

"Good," he mumbled, his fingers flying across his keyboard. "Productive. How was yours?" A passive tone settled into his words.

If I told him the truth would he even hear me? Or would I get a "That's good, honey"?

"It went well. The meeting was good. They are exquisitely talented. I booked them for the showing."

"That's good, honey."

I chuckled and started dinner.

After our evening routine, I had hoped he was up for a little sex. I could have used it after the day I had. Smiling, I tried setting the mood with a little nightie I found in the back of my closet. I hadn't worn it in a while. I walked into the bedroom where he sat on the end of the bed.

"I see someone is looking for a little sexy time tonight."

"After the day I've had, it would be a good stress reliever." I stopped in front of him and straddled him, his hands sliding up my legs.

"Well, I think I could manage a little loving myself." He patted my butt which told me to get into the normal position we made love in.

I tried kissing him with my legs still around him, moving my groin over his.

"Come on," he insisted. "Climb up into bed. I'll join you in just a few minutes."

I exhaled and did as he wanted. He disappeared into the bathroom and I heard water running, then the sound of a toothbrush in his mouth. When he climbed into bed his arm wrapped around me. He rubbed my stomach with his hands and spooned me from behind. I ran my fingers along his arm until his cock pushed into my backside. He rolled me onto my back and climbed on top, pushing my legs apart. When he pushed his dick inside me my pussy immediately tightened around him.

"Someone is worked up, isn't she?" He moved back and forth and planted little kisses on my mouth that deepened as we fucked. I wanted to devour him, or Malcolm, or someone, but too much was a turn-off for Ronald, so I suppressed my desire and let him do me as he did.

He moved back and forth with a rhythm and my arousal was building nicely. His face was buried in the crook of my neck which told me he was close, but then he stopped and picked up his head.

"What's wrong?" I asked, trying to pull him back to me.

"Shhh. I heard footsteps or something in the other room."

I looked out the bedroom door into the hallway and listened intently. "I don't hear anything," I whispered.

~HIM~

I pulled back out of the doorway just in time. She didn't see me. Giving it a couple of seconds, I listened for the repetitious movement of the bed again before peeking back into the room. She was so sexy laying there getting fucked, but it made me question why she was with him. He didn't treat her the way she needed to be treated. She was wasting her sexuality and I was going to show her the difference.

I watched her body as she moved back and forth underneath him, and my dick hardened in my jeans. My buddy tried to get my attention, but I waved him off. I think he was about as impatient as I was. Soft moaning came from the bedroom and I knew it wasn't gonna be long before we had to interrupt them. I grabbed myself and adjusted it to the side before leaning against the doorway waiting for her to see me watching them.

The moment her eyes locked onto mine, my cock lunged forward enough to tell me to get in there and take over. It excited me to see the fear in her eyes because I was going to change that to hunger. I was going to change that to lust. I was going to change her for me.

~HER~

Ronald planted his lips on mine for a few seconds as he started his rhythm again, then buried his face into my neck.

A noise much like he described came from the other room and I glanced toward the door again. This time I saw movement and a man with a black mask appeared just outside the doorway, his covered head peeking into the room. Panic rushed through me and I tapped Ronald on the arm. "Someone is watching us." I barely whispered and wondered if he even heard me as he picked up his rhythm. "Ronald," I whispered louder.

"One second," he grunted.

I pushed him off me and grabbed at the covers, my eyes wide and staring at three hooded men as they walked into the room.

"Ronald, is it?" one of the men said. "Oh, my man. Is that any way to treat such a lovely creature?"

"Who are you and what are you doing in my house? Get out, before I call the cops," he demanded.

"I don't think you'll be doing any of that." The same man spoke as they surrounded the bed.

My heart pounded against the inside of my chest and I could barely breathe as I clutched the blanket tight to my chest.

"What *are* we doing in his house?" the man asked the taller of the three.

"I thought we were just going to take a few things, but after seeing this, we can't just leave without fixing the situation."

"I agree." The two men high-fived each other.

"What... are you talking about?" Ronald climbed up onto his knees, not caring what he exposed. "Get out, now!"

"Oh, my dear Ronald. You are in no position to be barking orders, especially since we are here to help you."

The taller man, I'll call him Stretch, walked to Ronald's side of the bed and grabbed his arms from behind, while the spokesman of the trio helped detain him as he struggled to break free.

I tried to scream, but nothing would produce from my tightened throat. I was shaking in fear as I watched Stretch remove his belt. His eyes were glued to me, but he buckled it around Ronald's waist, bounding his arms to his side. "Now sit!" The spokesman demanded. "My colleagues and I are going to show you how you should be fucking your wife."

"What-what are you talking about?" Ronald's voice shook.

"I'm talking about an unhappy wife with all the right equipment and no way to express herself freely." His eyes glided down my body. "I'm going to give you a little sex education 101 my dear boy."

"You're going to rape my wife?"

"No. Not at all. In fact, I won't even touch her until she asks me to."

"We should get paid for this kind of teaching." The third one finally spoke up. I'll call him Three.

"I agree." Stretch went to the nightstand and picked Ronald's wallet up. Opening it, he pulled what money Ronald had and waved it in the air. "This doesn't look like it's enough to cover our services." He shoved it back into the wallet and went back and stood next to Ronald still sitting on the floor.

"Please. Just go," he pleaded. "Take whatever you want and get the hell out."

"Oh, we will." The spokesman smiled through his mask and approached the bed toward me.

I shook my head violently and pushed myself against the headboard. "I'll never...."

"Don't make a decision so quickly, my beauty." He stared at me and the panic that seized me subsided. There was something about his eyes, they calmed me. "You need this, don't you?" he said.

My body reacted with the same arousal I felt when I caught Malcolm watching me masturbate in the gallery. I couldn't deny it. I did need this.

"Think about it. Someone else's cock inside you, strange hands doing things to your body you have only fantasized about until now. It could all be yours."

I glanced at Ronald and loosened the grip on my blanket.

"Don't worry about your husband. He'll be on board before the night is through. I promise you."

I licked my lips as a euphoria swept over me. I lowered the blanket and glanced at Ronald again, a twinge of guilt sliding in before looking back at the man standing by the bed.

Stretch patted Ronald on the shoulder and glued his eyes on my tits. "Watch and learn, my man."

The spokesman unbuckled his belt and pulled it from his blue jeans. He doubled his cock in his hand and ran his fingers up and down on it. "Tell me, Vicky."

My name on his lips jolted me. "You know me?" Panic was in my voice.

"No. Your man here called out your name while he was making sweet, boring love to you."

I didn't recall him doing that, but it didn't make it a lie. Right? I looked up at the man moving toward me and swallowed hard.

"Tell me what you want." He licked his lips and I started to tremble. "Tell me to leave and you'll never see me again."

I glanced again at Ronald and shook my head slightly. "Touch me," I whispered.

"What was that?"

I inhaled deeply and repeated my words louder. "I want you to touch me."

"Let the games begin," he smirked.

He leaned over the bed and lassoed his belt around my back pulling it tight. I gasped at the cool leather against my bare skin. My arms stayed loose at my sides as he pulled me toward him, me obliging as I climbed to my knees and walked myself to the edge of the bed in front of him. His gloved hand ran across my tits and the smell of leather wafted into my senses as he snaked his arm around me. He pressed himself against my naked body, his jeans rough against my thighs. He lowered his hand to my ass and pulled me into him, his bulging cock straining against his jeans. He was big, as big as Ronald was, but he wasn't going to treat me like Ronald did, and that absolutely thrilled me.

My pussy ached for him to touch me there. And he did. His gloved hand moved around my thigh and pushed my legs apart before rubbing across my lips. He leaned down and devoured my mouth with his, his tongue pushing through my lips and filling my mouth. He inhaled deeply as his finger pushed inside my pussy. The leather was rough inside of me but excited me further. He fingered me with his leather glove and the roughness almost made me cum right on the spot.

He pulled out and pushed me back onto the bed, shaking his head and his finger in the air. "Not yet, my little slut."

His new name for me made me tremble with excitement as he pulled the glove off his hand with his teeth. His skin was dark and that thrilled me even more. I was going to get fucked in front of my husband by a black man.

He lowered his jeans and stroked his massive cock, smiling as he watched me tremble. "You want this bad, don't you?" He grabbed a handful of himself and shook it in front of me.

I nodded. It was all I could do.

He glanced up at Three and I looked over toward him. Stretch still stood next to Ronald as Three walked to the other side of the bed. He took my arms in his hands and pulled them over my head, his weight shifting forward. This was it. My fantasy was becoming a reality and everything I experienced inside that morning was nothing compared to what I was experiencing during the real thing.

"Open your legs for me and show me that pretty pussy."

"Oh, God!" Ronald spat. "Victoria! Don't do this!" He struggled to get up but Stretch kept him where he sat.

I directed my attention forward and positioned myself on my back for the man standing in front of me. I opened my legs, as Three held my arms down on the mattress. All they had to do was fondle me a little bit and I would have exploded.

The man stroking his cock climbed onto the bed over the top of me and devoured my mouth, his demanding tongue pushing in and making me dizzy. My breathing was hard and labored the moment he stopped exploring my mouth almost choking me with his tongue. He dragged it over my chin and down my neck, biting my skin as he lowered himself further. Before his mouth sucked my nipple in, Three took over kissing me and blocked my sight from watching what was happening to me. His tongue delved into my mouth a little more delicately. His hands slid up my arms as heavy wet smooches trailed down my stomach. My legs were forced apart and his mouth consumed my pussy lapping at my folds, something pushing inside me.

I was breathing so hard my mouth became dry. My entire body trembled uncontrollably. I had forgotten where I was until I caught a glimpse of Ronald tied helplessly to our oversized desk in the corner. Stretch had secured him with something and was walking to the bed, pulling his shirt off as he walked closer.

Oh, God! Three men at the same time!

"This looks fun," he said before climbing onto the bed beside me. "Mind if I join you?" His hand caressed my tits, and his mouth began trailing around my nipple. "Want to join in on the fun, Ronald?" He looked back at my struggling husband, red in the face and a cock so hard he couldn't hide it. "Not yet?" Stretch chuckled. "You let us know. I'm sure your wife would love it if you joined us."

The man was right. I would have, but at that moment I couldn't request much. I was dizzy with desire and my body ached with pleasure.

Three positioned himself on the right side of me as Stretch hovered over me on the right. My big black lover had his hands on my knees and was sliding them up and down my thighs, his beautiful cock pushing against my pussy. He leaned forward spreading my opening wide and agonizingly slowly he inched his way inside me. "You taking notes, Ronald?" he asked, not taking his eyes off what he was doing. "This is how you truly pleasure your wife. This is what she really wants." He pushed inside further and grunted. "Fuck! You're tight."

My pussy stretched around his cock and as he worked it back and forth, I felt the pressure build. Thumbs were rubbing over my nipples. A tongue filled my mouth. Hands were squeezing my breasts and fingers were rolling over my clit. Meanwhile, my mind was completely clouded, my body responded with every flick, bite, and lick and I couldn't hold back my orgasm any longer. I turned my head away from the mouth that devoured it and screamed as every muscle seized up and an orgasm hit me like a boulder. It held on and shook me for several moments before letting me go.

The massive black cock was still rocking in and out of me, the man between my legs grunting and gripping at my thighs. His grunts got louder and quicker, his thrusts went deeper and harder and when he pulled himself out, he flooded my stomach with his semen. Three had his cock in his hand and was stroking himself until it was apparently his turn. He took my hands and sat me up, motioning me to my knees. He directed me toward Ronald before lowering me onto my hands so I had to look up at him and he would see the whole show. I couldn't look at him, but I didn't want this to stop either. I rubbed my sensitive clit as Three slapped his hand on my asscheek over and over again. It began to sting but he'd rub it in between the slaps causing pleasure to seep into my pussy. I ached for him to be inside me.

"Tell me what you want," he said.

I trembled. I loved this. "I want you to fuck me."

"You can do better than that. Slut."

The term ripped through me. "I want to feel your cock inside me, pushing into me and claiming my pussy."

"Mmmm. Yes. Better." He slapped my asscheek. Pain searing over my skin. "Look up at your husband, slut."

The black man stood to the side, his jeans up but still undone. Stretch sat next to me, his hands cradling my tits over the mattress. His fingers fondled them slowly as he stroked himself. By this time, I was so aroused it wasn't going to take long to feel that next orgasm, something I had never done. Two orgasms in a night would be my first.

I looked up at Ronald, his face distorted but his dick hard as a rock. He was staring at my body and what they were doing to it. He liked this, too. Maybe he could be next. Four men fucking me in one night. I shivered in delight and pushed back into Three until the head of his dick opened me up. He slapped my ass again, grabbed my hips, and pushed himself into me with one thrust. I gasped hard. He filled me quickly and fucked me, my body jarring forward with each thrust. Stretch climbed off the bed and went to Ronald's side. He was whispering something in his ear and Ronald was nodding. He didn't seem so distraught and I wondered what he was telling him.

Stretch untied him and he approached me with his dick in his hand. Stretch grabbed a handful of my hair and positioned my head. I immediately knew what it was for and I squirmed with excitement at the thought.

"I had no idea," Ronald said, his eyes hungry. He stroked himself and stood before me. I opened my mouth for him as Three slowly fucked me from behind, his thumb stroking my other hole. Ronald stopped in front of me and I welcomed his cock with the tip of my tongue. As it eased into my mouth, I could feel the bulging veins along the sides, and I leaned forward to tighten my mouth over him. I sucked on it and twirled my tongue around his head trying to watch his face as I did. He was staring at the cock that was fucking me so good, his mouth falling open.

Three picked up his speed and slammed into me repeatedly, my nipples dragging along the blankets underneath me. Everything I was experiencing at one time all balled up inside me and a second orgasm exploded without warning. Ronald got aggressive and grabbed my hair, shoving his dick deeper into my mouth. It hit the back of my throat and pushed further until he was stroking my throat with it.

Three grunted a few times and pulled out before a wad of semen squirted up my back. Ronald pulled out of my mouth and I collapsed onto the bed.

"Don't tell me you're done," said Stretch. "What about us?" He slid his arm around Ronald's neck and smiled. He rolled me to my back and pulled me to the edge of the bed until my ass was on the edge. "Are you ready for more cock, baby?"

Amativeness tickled me again and the idea I was their sex toy titillated me. I shivered again and nodded.

He waited for Ronald to straddle my chest and lean forward, pushing his cock back into my mouth before he entered me and started fucking me. He wasn't as big as the others, but I still had no problem feeling another orgasm deep down threatening to slam me again. I opened my legs, and he pushed my knees to my armpits around Ronald. He leaned forward, pushing my legs down further, and bobbed his ass up and down over me as his dick drilled in and out like I was an oil well.

I supposed with all of the previous excitement he was already so horny that it didn't take him long to shudder and cum inside me. Moments later Ronald did the same but in my mouth. I swallowed repeatedly holding my breath in between to avoid choking on it.

Stretch climbed off the bed and high-fived the spokesman as Ronald climbed over to me and kissed me passionately for the first time in a long time. "I want to fuck you," he whispered. "Wherever you want to go, whenever you want to do it."

I glanced around the room at the group of them, feeling so surreal and satisfied. "So, who gets the shower first?" I teased.

That night had rebirthed Ronald and our sex life has been on fire ever since. We never talked about what happened that night, but we also didn't admit that it was the reason we now try new things and new positions. My stress level has dropped considerably and when the day of the show came, I was more than ready.

After a long session of sex in the shower, Ronald and I had breakfast together and left the apartment at the same time. He squeezed my ass before climbing into his car and wished me luck on my show.

My gallery was beautiful and the pieces on display were sure to sell. When the artists arrived, I walked them through the itinerary and let them know that if they had any questions they could ask at any time. Several customers walked through the gallery during the course of the day and conversed with the artists. At the end of the day, I was exhausted but happy.

Aaron approached me with a smile. "What a successful day. How did we do?"

"We sold several pieces. I think we made over a hundred and fifty thousand."

"Very nice," he exclaimed with a nod. "Let's set up a meeting tomorrow evening?"

"Sounds perfect. I'll bring some wine and we can celebrate."

"Perfect." He smiled oddly at me before walking toward the front door.

"Congratulations," Malcolm said, approaching me.

"Thank you. To you as well. You have some beautiful pieces here."

"As do you." His eyes sunk into mine and it stirred something inside me. "I have just one question." The fact that he saw me masturbate was still fresh in my mind, but I wasn't going to make a deal out of it, especially after my new sexual awakening. This was my career, and we were professionals. I'd hoped he treated me with the same respect.

"What is your question?"

"How's your husband doing? Ronald? Is it?"

I froze and stared at him. I never introduced him to Ronald. I had never even brought up his name, or the fact that I was married. Ever since I lost my wedding ring a year ago, I was afraid to wear it. So that meant....

He walked away, pulling a pair of leather gloves from his pocket. He put them to his mouth and inhaled.

"Oh, one more thing?" he said, turning toward me. "Bring him to the meeting tomorrow night. I'd like to see him again."

~CHAPTER 3~

Fantasy BDSM Turned into Reality

Not Such a Stranger – She goes to a bar in NYC. He lives there somewhere. She doesn't know where. All she knows is his first name and several stories he used to tell her over the internet and telephone. She was addicted to him, but she had no idea who he was, until that night. She remembers the bar he mentioned frequently in his stories. And that night, she was about to become one of those stories. He knows her right away. He approaches her to thank her for being his muse, for being there to tell his stories to, for making him cum each time he spoke to her. He asks one final request. "I've imagined you so many times. I want to smell you on my fingers. Just one time." She allows it and he slides his hand up her skirt and into her panties. Removing his fingers, he intoxicates himself on her scent and begs for one more feel. She allows him and he keeps his fingers there until she's ready to cum herself. He demands that she move to the bathroom down the back hall. They end up in his apartment close by, with his playroom and many other exciting activities waiting for her.

I called the phone number again. And again, it rang busy. I couldn't understand it. How many times over the course of a year had I called this number? Rarely did he not answer, but never have we been disconnected for this long. Something was wrong, and I needed to know what that was. I needed to hear his voice. I needed to feel his words in my ears again. They'd seep into me like honey and devour my imagination, my mind, my sexual appetite.

I looked up his phone number in my emails from a year ago just to be sure I was dialing it right. I was beside myself. Did he change his phone number? Was he done with me? My mind raced back to the last conversation we had. He couldn't have been done with me. Our last forty-five-minute call was intense, highly erotic, and carnal. He often told me he could never go more than a few days without me. It had been over a week since I had spoken to him. Where was he?

I plopped down on my bed and reminisced about other conversations between us. I could never get personal with him and I could never ask to meet him. No 'I love you's' and no feelings could be talked about. It was strictly sex talk about experiences and dreams. But over the course of the year, I had put together bits and pieces of his life enough to know basically where he was. Not everything could be kept secret forever.

I slid my hands over my breasts thinking of him and a particular story he told me one evening when I was lying in my bed. It was late at night and I was almost asleep when my phone rang. It didn't matter when or where I was when I got his call. I found a way to answer, even if I couldn't say a word and had to listen only.

That night, he told me about a lover he had seduced in a museum around the corner from where he lived. It was a woman who knew what she wanted in life. She was strong, independent, and only needed a man for her sexual prowess, but when she met Robert her life changed.

He told me how he seduced her. He told me how she turned him down, and then he told me how he pursued her and won. By the time he got her into his bed she was so turned on by him that she became his play toy for months. Complete submission. I think she was married, but that didn't matter to Robert. What he wanted he got.

It made me wonder why he never pursued me. I was more than willing to do whatever he wanted. Yes, I was inexperienced, but I wanted him. One boyfriend and a few played-out fantasies were no match for the various women Robert has had. It wasn't because I wasn't attractive. I was always getting hit on. I was just picky. My fantasies far exceeded my lack of daring to try new things. When I met Robert that all changed, in my head anyway. After late nights of his stories, no man seemed worthy enough to try out.

I remember one afternoon when he was with her, he called my phone. I was sitting at the coffee shop working on my thesis when his name scrolled across my screen. I hit the talk button and held it to my ear. Before I could say hello, I heard him grunt and strain his voice. I closed my mouth and I listened. He was fucking her, and he was very vocal about it. He described what was going on and he told me what she was doing to him in detail. I was so turned on by it that I left my things at the table and went into the ladies' room. I pushed my hand into my pants and started pleasuring myself in the bathroom stall. When he told me, her mouth wrapped around his cock and she strained to take him all in, I imagined every detail of what she must have looked like. When he yelled out in ecstasy, I mentally saw his head fall back as he pumped his organ in deeper. "I'm going to cum, Mia." He'd call my name out, not hers and it jolted me. "Mia!" His orgasm was so loud and guttural that I orgasmed immediately after he did.

I couldn't be in love with him, but I couldn't stop thinking about him. What he gave me kept me insatiable, kept me wanting, my mind looking for the next fantasy he'd spoon-feed me. I didn't know him, but I knew I didn't want it to end. My girlfriend, Sasha, put me on to this dating site a year ago and that's where I met him but I never dreamt it would turn into anything like this. What we had between us was different than anything I could imagine. It wasn't platonic. It wasn't traditional. It was hot and steamy, and I wanted more.

"Do you know what I think you should do?" Sasha sipped her mocha cappuccino, her eyes glued to mine.

"I don't know what I can do. I've tried everything I know. I've called him a hundred times. I've tried texting him. I went back to that website. He's gone. Vanished. And he took my libido with him."

"Go to New York."

I looked up at her like she slapped my face. "What?"

"Go to New York."

"I can't go to New York. Are you insane?"

"Why not?"

"I… I have school."

"It's your last year of college. I know your schedule. You can juggle shit around and make this work. Just go and find him. You don't have to be gone for a long time."

"It's over five hundred miles away. How the hell will I get there?"

"It's called a plane? I'll cover for you at the restaurant."

"I can't…."

"You're making excuses, Mia. You have to go. Otherwise, you'll drive yourself crazy."

My stomach started to ache with the idea I just might do it. Sasha saw it in my face and smiled.

"But what if…."

"Don't," she interrupted. "Don't 'what-if' anything. Just go. If you don't, you'll never know, and you'll hate yourself forever."

I sighed, the ache in my stomach increasing. "I think I might puke."

"He's a New Yorker with a massive sex drive." She rolled her eyes. "Not some massively famous celebrity."

"How do we know that?" I waited for her to respond. "How do we know who he is? There's got to be some reason he has never webcammed with me or sent me a picture of him. Every time I ask him something about his life, he tells me another story and gets me all worked up again."

"I know. I'm so jealous."

"He knows what I look like. He knows everything about me. He could have had me killed by now if that was his thing, but since it's been over a year, I think I'm safe from that. He's probably married."

"Or has a girlfriend who doesn't put out how he likes."

"Maybe he's a she in disguise and he's afraid to tell me."

"Maybe he's ugly."

"It doesn't matter what he looks like."

"Obviously." She rolled her eyes. "I don't know what this guy has done to you, Mia. But you need to go."

"How would I even find him?"

"You know where he hangs out. He talked about MOMA and the subway. What's the name of that one bar he always mentions?"

"Ophelia's Lounge."

"Okay." She picked up her phone, her fingers flying over the keys. "Here." She turned the screen to me. "Write this down."

It was the address to Ophelia's Lounge in New York City.

"Go there and get drunk. Let him find you."

"And what if...."

"Mia. What did I tell you? No 'what-ifs'. Just go."

I nodded quickly and gathered my things together. I was going to do it. I was going to fly to New York to find a man I had never met. I couldn't allow myself to think beyond that. I'd talk myself out of going.

An hour after boarding the plane I wanted to turn back. I wanted to abort the mission and go back to my apartment. I wanted to forget about Robert and what he had done to my sexual appetite over the course of a year.

"Excuse me." A man's voice a few rows up from where I sat stopped the stewardess. It was familiar and it piqued my interest. "Do you have any wine? I would like white if you have it."

"I'm sorry Sir. We don't serve alcohol on this flight since it is only an hour flight. I apologize for any inconvenience. If you would like something else, I can get that for you."

"Just a bottle of water would be fine. Thank you."

"Of course."

I stared at the back of the man's head, my eyes wide. His voice. It couldn't be. Could it? I opened my phone, went to my voicemails, and listened to one of his messages. It was the one where he told me he needed me, but I wasn't there. It was the one he told me he was disappointed because he couldn't get a hold of me and he wanted to tell me a story. He told me he was rock hard and needed to hear my voice to cum for me. Since the day I met him, he has told me many stories, some fictitious, some true according to him. I didn't know what to expect when and if I got face-to-face with him, but Sasha was right. I needed to find out who he was and why he was so secretive. This man was more than just sex over the phone. He has gotten to me. He has gotten into my mind, into my consciousness, and into my mental state. I couldn't just walk away and forget everything about him.

I stared at the man a few rows up and listened to Robert's message again. What were the chances it was him? Maybe he flew to Ohio to find me and he was headed back to New York. Stranger things have happened, right?

I gripped the chair and pushed myself up to my feet. I needed to ask him something, anything, just to hear his voice. But when I moved into the aisle, a woman came from the bathroom the opposite way and kissed him on the cheek before squeezing by him. She sat in the seat next to him, her smile wide and her eyes twinkling. I plopped back down in my seat and watched them.

When the plane finally landed, and everybody climbed off I followed the couple as they walked through the terminals in the airport. They had met up with another couple who was welcoming them with open arms and small children clinging to their legs. I merely smiled at their happy reunion and walked away, satisfied that he wasn't Robert, but upset that he wasn't.

Pulling the notebook out of my bag I looked at the address I wrote down for Ophelia's Lounge and looked up a hotel close by. The Millennium Hilton just around the block was to be my home for the next few nights at least. It was a gorgeous hotel for the price. Not too expensive for Manhattan.

By that evening, I was settled into my room, freshly clean and dressed and I was sitting at the bar Robert had mentioned more than once in his stories and conversations. I ordered a drink and took a sip. I was in his world and honestly, it scared the hell out of me. It made me question why I was pursuing him. I was always worried about him coming after me. He knew enough about me to make it happen. Never did I ever, in a million years, think I'd be stalking him.

I was uneasy as I looked around at the faces. Everyone was with someone else, conversing, business, potential love interest. I sat alone at the end like I was waiting for someone. He wasn't expecting me. He had no idea I was here, but was he? My eyes went from one face to another. I could have been looking right at him but how would I know?

I saw elements he had described to me while we talked over the phone. There was the corner booth hidden partially behind a large pillar wall. He had seduced a young woman and made her orgasm right there. He had left that evening with her underwear in his pocket and her scent on his tongue. I carried my drink to that booth and slid into the seat. I ran my hand over the soft material that wrapped the seat and wondered where she sat when she came. Euphoria filled me and arousal hinted deep inside. He sat here next to her with his hand up her dress and when the bar closed, he tipped the bartender enough to keep his lover there afterward. He bent her over the back of the booth, her face pressed against the window and he fucked her. I ran my hand along the back of the booth and felt the heat spread through me. A couple walked by me and stared long enough to question what the hell I was doing, so I got up and went to another part of the bar.

Lower square stools lined a window that overlooked a beautiful skyline and each stool had white fur covering each one. My mouth fell slightly open as I walked to one of them and ran my hand across it. My mind went back to a conversation ... a story.

Robert had followed a woman out of the museum, and she led him here. She flirted with him terribly that day and he told her she wasn't going to get away with it. This was where she sat when he told her, or demanded rather, that she remove her bra and her underwear and hitch up her dress to sit bare-bottomed on the fur. He wanted them as a memento of their night together. He sat close to her and told her to touch herself. He wanted to watch her cum for him. He told me that he stole the fur and kept it for a souvenir to remember her by. The thought thrilled me, and I wanted one for myself. Maybe I would take one before I left back to Ohio as a souvenir of his story that stuck in my mind.

After a few more drinks and a full tour of the place with my eyes and my mind, I was convinced I wasn't going to see him that night. I sat back at the bar, finished my drink, and slid it forward. Before I got up another one was sitting in front of me. "Excuse me , I did not order this."

"Compliments of the gentleman at the table." He motioned toward a table and my heart picked up its pace. I pulled the drink closer and ran my finger up the side of the glass. Was it him? What would he look like? What would I say to him? I turned my head toward the table where an elderly gentleman sat with a smile on his face. My heart sank.

I raised my glass to him to thank him, praying that it was not the man I was looking for. He approached me and took the stool next to me.

"Good evening, young lady." The moment he spoke I smiled. It wasn't him. "I hope you don't mind my intrusion, but I just had to say hello. You look so much like my daughter before she moved away some years ago. I hope that's okay?"

"Oh, I don't mind at all."

He was a sweet old man, and he made my night not so terrible after all. He told me about the city and recommended a few places I should visit before I leave. I conversed with him over a couple more drinks before politely excusing myself for the night, thanking him again for being so nice.

The next day I walked around the city and imagined Robert close by. I visited the Museum of Modern Art. I walked in Central Park next to the water. Every man I passed I looked at twice, wondering if his name was Robert with a Jewish Jersey accent, wondering if his thoughts were full of the women he had seduced, wondering if he was looking for his next mission. Several of them I asked for directions to places I didn't plan on going, only to listen to their voices. His was distinct. Jewish. Dominating. Sexy. Smooth.

That evening I went back to Ophelia's and sat in the corner booth, then at the bar. I hoped that he would have visited and recognized me, but to no avail. I did the same the night after that and the night after that until I was about ready to give up.

"Excuse me." I got the bartender's attention as he walked by. "I'd like a glass of wine, please. And I have a question. I wondered if you could help me."

"I will try. What is it you want to know?"

"I'm supposed to meet someone here but I'm not sure what he looks like. Do you know a man named Robert that supposedly comes in here often?"

"I'm sorry, I don't. If he doesn't show and you'd like to leave a note for him I will be more than happy to give it to him. But most people usually let it go when they get stood up. Some even call them. Texting works, too."

His sarcasm was thick and blatant.

"Thanks."

"Any time."

I glanced around the room feeling defeated. I pulled my phone from my clutch and called Sasha.

"Tell me you have some news," she said before so much as a hello.

"I'm afraid I don't. I've been in Ophelia's every night since I got here and nothing. I even asked about him."

"And?"

"All I got was typical New York sarcasm. It's no use. I'm going to come back home tomorrow."

"I think you should hang out."

"These people here are beginning to think I'm either casing the joint or I'm pathetically lonely. I don't like drinking alone. You know that."

"Then hook up with one of those fine city boys. I hear New Yorkers know how to treat a woman right. Rough and hard."

"Sasha. I'm not hooking up with some random stranger."

"But you'll hold out for one you know has been around? You are an odd little bird."

"Thanks for the support."

"I love you, Mia. You know that. But, seriously, girl. You need some dick. Stay there and do some investigating work. You'll find him."

"And what if I don't?"

"Hopefully someone will pass by that feels sorry for you and he'll take care of you."

"You're a big help."

"I try."

"I will see you tomorrow."

"Suit yourself. Talk soon." She smooched twice into the phone before ending the call.

I gave a heavy sigh before finishing my drink and sliding the glass forward. The bartender had already filled another one and was headed toward me.

"No, thank you," I said, holding my hand up. "I'm going back to my hotel room."

"The gentleman behind you bought this one for you. You wouldn't want to disappoint, would you?"

I smiled, expecting to see the old man again, but when I turned around, it was someone different. He looked at me with an odd stare and a quirky smile upon his face, and he didn't say a word.

"Thank you, for the drink."

He nodded and cocked his head. "I've seen you in here a few times lately." His voice was low and controlled. "Where are you from?"

"What makes you think I'm from anywhere? There are eight million people living here."

"I overheard you on the phone. You're here visiting, aren't you?"

"Yes," I replied softly, concentrating on his tone. "And what about you?"

"I'm a native born and raised." There were hints of Robert's tone in the man's voice, but I couldn't confirm anything, nor did I dare. "May I?" He motioned toward the barstool next to me.

I didn't want him that close, but I wanted him there. He gave off the same energy Robert gave me. I felt myself nod.

Instead of sitting, he moved the stool over and rested his arms on the side of the bar as he sipped what I presumed to be bourbon or whiskey. His eyes stayed forward as if he were contemplating what to say to me.

I studied his features discreetly, his dark curls messed on top of his head, his pale skin against his icy blue eyes. He dressed superbly with a dark blue dress shirt underneath a black suit coat and black pants. Armani, maybe. He was awkward, but his confidence gave him this sex appeal that was alluring and charming.

"What is your name?" I asked, my eyes glued to his lips.

"Why do you ask?"

"I'd like to properly thank you for my drink."

He grinned and turned around, leaning his back against the bar as he redirected his focus toward the back of the bar. "It is me who should be thanking you."

I crossed my legs as my skirt fell away a bit exposing my thigh. "How so?" I felt sexy, like I was fitting in. Even if this wasn't Robert, I liked the way it was going.

His finger dragged across my knee, his eyes watching as it did. "I'd like you to do something for me. A favor of sorts."

My instinct was to pull back, but I remembered what Sasha said. I needed more in my life. *Dick,* as she had put it. "What sort of favor?"

"Allow me access to you."

I chuckled smugly and drew in a breath. "Access?"

"Yes. Open your legs."

My breath hitched. It was him. Undeniably. I drew in a quivering breath and tried to maintain my composure. "What do you mean?" I knew exactly what he meant. I needed time to calculate what was happening. My entire New York City experience up until that moment was long and dragged out. It all piled up and suffocated me and I needed to dig my way out.

He turned his head toward me and his eyes penetrated mine. He lowered his face, demanding my attention. "I want to smell you on my fingers, taste you on my tongue."

My face flooded with heat. "Um. What?"

"Isn't that why you're here, Mia?"

I shuddered at the sound of my name on his lips.

"To experience what I gave you online? When you didn't hear from me for a while you desired me more, didn't you? You craved my words in your ears. You needed to feed your addiction of me."

"I don't think so," I forced a smirk, my face flooded with heat. "I'm not *addicted* to you, or any man."

"I think you're wrong. Why else would you have come? You can't get enough of me, can you?"

"Excuse me?"

Was I wrong all this time? This wasn't the confident, sexy man I talked with online. He was arrogant and cocky, and I was second-guessing myself for pursuing him.

"Why else would you be sitting here alone, in a dress like that, exposing yourself to any man with the description in your head?"

"This was a mistake. You're not who I thought you were. I'm sorry. I have to go." I climbed off the barstool and turned to go.

"You've been here every night this week looking for me."

I looked back at him, annoyed more than anything. "You knew I was here? Why didn't you...?"

"I wasn't sure it was you at first. But I watched you. When you soaked up the atmosphere in the corner over there," he said without looking or motioning toward the booth. "You wanted to feel what she felt, didn't you?"

My annoyance dissipated quickly. I couldn't stop staring at him.

"And the white covers on the seats in the back? Did you lift your dress to feel it on your naked skin? Did you masturbate and soil them?"

I swallowed hard. "Why didn't you…?"

"Because I like watching you, Mia." He picked up my drink and held it out to me.

I accepted it and took my seat again.

"This addiction doesn't stop at you. You have become a drug to me as well. Your reactions to my experiences. I find myself craving the next time I can hear your voice."

"Then why did you stop? It has been a week."

"Life happens. It's not always fun and games. I had some things I had to tend to."

"A wife?" Annoyance threatened me again.

"Nothing concerning to you, and nothing that would hurt someone else." He moved closer, this time turning his entire body toward me. "You need to trust me." His finger dragged along my leg again. "Allow me access, Mia." His words were barely audible but close to my ear, and the heat from his mouth sent a shiver down my side. "Just a touch," he whispered. "Right here."

His fingertips sliding up the inside of my thigh drew my hunger out. My heart hit steadily against my chest. My fingertips felt cold to the touch. My mouth went dry, but….

"I know you're wet, Mia." He inhaled a full breath, his nose gliding through my hair. "Let me. Touch you. Just a moment's touch will give me everything I need."

I nodded, my mouth slightly open, my breathing shallow, small. I was rigid, staring at the fingernail on my thumb attached to my hand that wrapped tightly around my drink on the bar.

"You aren't like the women in my life." The palm of his hand rested against my thigh and inched closer to my heat, my wet, my ache. "I fuck them, Mia. I always tell you the details. We share my experiences, and I like that. I like explaining my pursuit and my conquer. I like that you listen and you cum." He emphasized the last word as his hand brushed against my pussy. "My only regret is not being able to smell you, to taste you. I have craved this for so long."

My breath caught in my throat, my eyes looking around the room nervously.

"No one is watching. No one has a clue. It's just you and I here right now. In this moment. Give it to me, Mia."

I leaned forward in my seat and opened my legs, my hand clutching my drink a little harder. My eyes closed to enjoy the move of his hand up to the elastic on my panties. He pushed inside and slid his hand across until it covered my pussy completely. I could hear him take a deep breath and slowly exhale. His fingers moved slightly, then entered me, pushing inside. I glanced up at his face. His eyes were closed. His head was bent back slightly. His mouth barely opened. I imagined how this story would go over the phone as he told it to me on a late night. Very heated, very stimulating, much like now.

He withdrew his hand and lifted it to his face. He attempted another deep breath, but it caught. He held it in. He slid his finger into his mouth and sucked on it, his eyes still closed. Fire raced through me as I stared at him.

"My God, Mia." His hand rested on the small of my back. "You're so fucking intoxicating." His hand rested on my thigh again. He stood there not moving, his head down and his eyes still closed.

What was he doing? What was he thinking?

"May I? Once more?" He opened his eyes and watched my face.

I opened my legs slightly, glancing at the others around us still consumed by their own surroundings.

His hand rested against the inside of my thigh, inching closer. His fingers snaked underneath the elastic and crept inside until they were positioned against my heat once again. This time he stayed, his fingers slipping inside me. He moved them in and out agonizingly slowly.

"What are you doing?" I whispered, grabbing his wrist between my legs.

"I needed what you just gave to me. You were so incredible in giving it to me. Now, I'm giving what you need from me."

"No," I whispered. "Don't. Not here."

"Shall we go to the corner?" His grin was devious, his hand moved against me, his fingers spreading my desire further. "Let me," he barely said, his lips close to my ear.

I scooted to the end of my seat and took in a ragged breath, opening my legs a little further before he continued.

"Good girl."

He finger fucked me slowly and I concentrated on appearing as calm as I could. He rubbed his thumb through my lips.

"Ugh." I slammed my mouth closed and looked around. My legs closed around his hand. I was a little louder than I should have been. I faked clearing my throat and pretended to laugh at something he would have said if he wasn't finger fucking me in a bar in the middle of New York City with patrons around us.

Robert chuckled, his hand still in place but not moving.

"Sorry." Heat flooded my face, and I downed the rest of my drink.

His fingers began to move only after I opened my legs for him.

"Would you like another drink?" The bartender had a smile on his face that one couldn't pry off with a crowbar. He did know Robert and the kind of man he was. But I couldn't walk away. I was in too deep, and I wanted him deep inside me.

"Please," was all I could muster without feeding his suspicions.

Robert's fingers moved inside me deliciously until the people around us faded away. I opened further. I rocked in my seat to the rhythm of his hand caressing back and forth, his fingers inside me then roaming down to my anus, then back up and inside me again. The more he played the hotter I got, not caring about those around me who started suspecting that something more than conversation was going on between us.

"Go into the ladies' room."

"Why?"

"Because I don't feel like getting thrown out of here. Sex in a public place, although thrilling beyond life itself, is illegal."

"Oh." I glanced at eyes on us.

"When you're the only one inside, lock the door and wait for me." He withdrew his hand and turned away from me, one hand on his drink and the other under his nose. He inhaled deeply, closed his eyes, and sipped his drink. "Go."

I was in foreign territory and the next decision I made could be one of the most dangerous decisions, or it could be one of the most thrilling of my life. I didn't bother adjusting my underwear. When I climbed off my seat my skirt fell back to where it should have been, and I walked away from him. Whether I stayed in the ladies' room and waited for him, or pretended to and disappeared from his life, the decision needed to be made in the next few moments.

Walking in, there was one other woman inside. I went into a stall and thoughts of masturbating in a stall to his voice on the phone flooded my mind. I listened as the woman finished her business and went to the sink. The water flowed as I leaned against the stall door, my mind was all over the place, my body was on fire, my pussy ached. The door opened and I was alone. My heart raced. I left the stall and quickly washed my hands, pressing them against my face.

I didn't know this guy well enough to sleep with him. I was fine with thoughts of it. I was good with self-pleasure. I wasn't good with ending up dead or with some STD. I was worried that he had disappeared. I sought him out and I found him. He was fine. He wasn't gone at all. Life gets in the way. I looked at my image in the mirror and nodded as my decision was made. I was going to sneak out of there and go back to Ohio.

Two knocks following a third knock sounded on the other side of the door. I froze and my vaginal muscles contracted sending a tremble through me.

I didn't move, but the door did. It opened slowly and Robert walked in. He didn't ask me what my decision was. He didn't look to see if we were alone. He didn't say a word. The moment he saw me next to the sink he rushed toward me, his hand sliding around the back of my neck and his other hand grabbing my side. He pushed me up against the wall and his body pinned me there, heat pushing into me from every angle. The palm of his hand cupped my chin and forced my head up, his tongue running along my collarbone before biting at the side of my neck. He wiggled his hand up underneath my blouse and glided his hand up until it was full of lace and breast. He yanked the lace out of his way and rolled his fingers over my nipple sending electricity through me. His knee forced its way between my legs and pushed them apart as his hand fed its way down between. His mouth captured mine and the taste of whiskey spread over my tongue. He moaned into his throat sending vibrations through me bringing my orgasm slightly closer to reality.

I dove my fingers into those curls as he devoured my mouth, moving his tongue over my chin and feasting his way down my neck. His hand gripped my blouse and shoved it upward until I was exposed to him. He pulled my other breast free and pushed them together before indulging on my nipples.

My stomach trembled. My legs were weak, and my breathing was labored as he moved further down past my stomach, his hands still on my chest. He lowered himself to his knees and looked up at me, dropping his hands to his lap before looking forward at my skirt. His hands connected with the outside of my thighs and they moved upward taking the material of my skirt with them. He covered his head leaving me with nothing to watch but my own image in the mirror beside me. The woman looking back at me wasn't me. I had never seen her before in my life, but I was jealous of her. I wanted to become her. She was exciting, bold, daring, and Robert's lover. Did I dare?

His hands slid up my hips and hooked into the sides of my underwear pulling them down my legs and they pulled my barriers down with them. His hands appeared on the outside of my skirt gripping the sides of my waist. I concentrated on the large ring on his finger as his tongue slid between my lips. The hardened tip swirled around my clit causing my thoughts to swirl around in my head. I was breathing heavily while he lapped at my folds and pushed me closer to the orgasm that threatened to grab hold of me.

I grabbed at something along the wall, something to hold on to as pressure built inside me. I picked my leg up, waiting for the explosion to hit when he stopped and let go, pushing my skirt back down before he stood up in front of me. He kissed me hard, but his hands were nowhere to be found.

I reached for his pants, but he held my arms to the wall above my head. "Please," I cooed. "Don't stop. I'm so close."

He pulled himself away from me and stood there as if he were looking for a reaction.

My eyes widened. "What...what are you doing?'

"Patience, my sweet girl. I have a surprise for you."

"No. I don't want a surprise. I want to...."

He pushed his hand over my mouth and leaned himself into me. "Shhh. Not yet."

I could feel his hardened cock pressing into me and I wanted to rub against it. He kept my hands against the wall knowing I'd satisfy myself.

"Robert," I pleaded.

He pulled me off the wall and slid himself behind me, his arms holding me to him. I bent my head to the side when his mouth kissed my neck. I reached back to his thigh and slid my hand to his sizable cock, rubbing him through his pants. Maybe I could get him hot enough to not want to stop. I jerked him off through his pants until the door opened. I tried pulling away, but he held me tight where I stood.

"Robert," I whispered.

"Shhh."

A large black man walked into the ladies' bathroom and stood in front of us, his eyes greedy. He licked his lips and I pushed back into Robert. Was this my surprise? I was just getting to know the physical Robert and he wanted to introduce another cock into my life? I wasn't okay with this, was I?

"This your girl?" the man said, eyeing me up and down.

"Yes." Robert's voice was soft, velvety. "My wife has always wanted someone to watch me fuck her."

A surge of air forced its way into my lungs as excitement, fear, panic, and hysteria raced through my veins.

The man grabbed his crotch and smiled. "I think I can oblige her wishes. She's fucking gorgeous. Quite a sex pot, huh?"

"Very exotic." Robert pulled my hair away from my neck and kissed me there. "Are you ready?" he asked close to my ear.

I could barely speak. I was about to do something only Robert could think up in his stories. I was about to become one of his stories and the eroticism of it all hit me like a boulder.

He leaned down enough to grab my skirt and lift it to my waist. My underwear was still on the floor at my feet. The air hit me between my legs as the man in front of me took me in. He shook his head and licked his lips, his hand sliding up and down the front of his pants. "Man, I don't know if I can just watch this. You got yourself a *hot* little pussy there."

"Yes, I do." Robert's tone turned carnal and somewhere between his desire to showcase me to a stranger and that stranger's eyes on my bare pussy, his pants came off. His hands ran across my thighs and in between my legs as his dick pushed in between my ass cheeks. He humped me, his wetness slick along my ass and on my thighs. He grabbed my hair in his fist and gently pulled my head back as he pushed into me threatening to penetrate me. "Tell him what you want, darling."

Panic mixed with my desire and I set my sight on the man in front of me. He was stroking his cock that protruded from his open pants. His mouth hung open and he stared at my body. I was center stage and was asked to perform.

Truth was, this wasn't what I wanted. It was too much, and it frightened me. I wasn't about to admit such a defeat, so I pushed away from Robert and walked toward the other man. "I want him, and I want you to watch him fuck me." I spun around and grinned at Robert waiting for his response.

His eyes flashed with anger. His plan had backfired. I'd be damned if I was to be just another quest. "What about what we talked about?" he asked through gritted teeth.

"Well, you know I always get what I want. Darling." I was pushing it. I could see that, and it made me nervous, but it also thrilled me.

Robert reached down and pulled his pants back up, securing them around him. He stayed silent while he did so. Our new friend didn't know what to do. He had put himself back together after Robert's reaction. Did I push things too far? It seemed we were done there, and all plans were off.

Not another word was said when he reached down and scooped my panties off the floor shoving them into his pocket. He walked by his friend and unlocked the door. I smiled. I won. He would have his way with me alone in that bathroom. Or so I had thought. He whipped the door open, lunged at me, and seized my wrist with his hand, yanking me out of the room.

"Don't say a word," he commanded as he walked me out of the bar. No one looked up.

Once we were on the street I stopped and struggled against his grip. "You can let me go now. Your little skit is over."

He continued to pull me along behind him.

"Where are we going? Where are you...?"

He stopped and whipped around, pulling me into him. His hand gripped the back of my neck as his mouth smashed against mine. He thrust his tongue into my mouth and kissed me hard, while his other hand reached underneath my skirt and immediately found my pussy still wet from his cock. He pushed two fingers inside me and slammed them in and out of me until I was panting heavily. I gripped his jacket with both hands and held on. If he continued, I was going to orgasm right there on the street at the mercy of his hands. But he didn't. He pushed me to the brink of orgasm then stopped and held me there.

"Don't test me, Mia. I know much more than you do. I can create the most incredible orgasm you'll ever experience, or I can punish you and torment you until I decide your fate. Do you understand?"

I was still panting, my head dizzy, but I nodded.

"Nothing I do is for anyone else except for me. Don't ever forget that."

I nodded again, nervous that he was going to hurt me. I needed to get away from him, but I let him lead me along.

We had walked a couple of blocks then down a narrow alleyway before it opened up to a large empty parking lot. He led me through the dimly lit lot and stopped in the center, large buildings all around us.

He pulled me closer and cupped my face, looking down at me. His face was softer, calm. His kiss was tender. It melted me. "Do you trust me?"

It was a loaded question. Did I? I knew what he could do, and it fed my addiction for him but was it enough to allow him full access to do what he wanted? That was what this question meant when he asked it.

I nodded, swallowed hard, and licked my lips. My fingers felt cold. *I don't! I want to leave! I was wrong for coming here.* "I do."

His hand slithered into the pocket of his jacket and he produced a beautiful black scarf. He wrapped each end around his hands and held it tight in front of my face. I knew what it was for. My body trembled with so many emotions at the thought of giving up all control to him.

He walked behind me and lowered it over my head. He slid it across my neck and the silky feel provoked my arousal. He placed it over my eyes and pulled it tight, tying it behind my head.

I lightly touched it, accepting the dark and homing into my other senses. His hand slid into mine and he tugged me forward. I extended my other hand outward and scuffled my feet forward as he led me along.

"There are some stairs," he said quietly.

I tapped my foot forward and picked it up. I mentally counted as my foot raised up to each one. One, two, three, four, five, six, seven, eight, nine, ten, eleven. A buzzer, then the click of a door. The air became warmer as the door closed behind us. I followed, clutching onto his arm. We stopped. I heard my own breathing and nothing else until the ding of an elevator sounded. Doors opened and he led me forward. The drop of my stomach told me we were going up. I tried counting the floors, but it was impossible to tell how fast the elevator climbed.

When the doors opened again, Robert tugged me forward. A few hundred feet, a key in a lock and a door opened. The smell of roses and vanilla tickled my nose. It was pleasant, alluring. I inhaled and enjoyed the scent.

"Sit here." He was in front of me with his hands on my arms. I sat back, my hands finding the cushion of a chair or a sofa. "Leave your blindfold on."

I nodded and tried to relax. The air around me went quiet. No footsteps, no rustling around, no words. Nothing.

"Robert?" I listened intently. Nothing.

I didn't know how long I sat there alone in silence, but it was enough time to calm my arousal. I began questioning my decision to allow him to lead me to what I assumed was his apartment. If I left would he know?

Would I know how to get out of there? I didn't want to go, but I didn't want to sit in silence and wait for whatever was going to happen, either. The wait was worse than the whip. I craved Robert's hands on me, his mouth savoring me, his cock penetrating me. I leaned back to wait and sleep crept in.

When I awoke, I was lying out flat. A light blanket covered me. I jolted upright and wanted to tear the blindfold off.

"Hey, sleepyhead." Robert's voice came from somewhere in front of me.

I lightly touched the blindfold still intact. "I fell asleep?"

"You did."

"For how long?"

"Quite a while."

"Why didn't you wake me?"

"I want you rested. Calm. Ready."

I heard the clink of glass next to me.

"Open your mouth. Do you like strawberries?"

I nodded, opening my mouth as directed and a sweet berry entered my lips. I bit down at the succulent taste and allowed it to spread across my palate. He fed me the rest and then another before setting them aside.

"There will be more for you later. You'll have quite an appetite when we are done."

Sensation tickled between my legs. I jumped when his hands took mine and he pulled me to my feet.

"This way, my sweet."

He pulled me along and a door closed. I heard running water. The scarf loosened and was lifted away from my eyes. I blinked excessively as they adjusted to the light. Robert stood in front of me in a white dress shirt unbuttoned enough to expose part of his chest. His sleeves were loose around his arms and it hung loosely over his black dress pants. He was sexy as hell.

He leaned into a large shower with glass walls and adjusted the water. I looked around the spacious bathroom. It was luxurious and beautiful. A gift bag sat on the counter with a toothbrush sticking up out of it.

"There are garments on the shelf for you to wear after you shower. Toiletries in the small bag by the sink. Replace your blindfold when you are finished with everything. I will be back in when you are ready."

"How will you know when I'm ready?"

He didn't respond. He merely left the room and closed the door behind him. I looked around the large room, steam collecting up by the ceiling. There was no clock and somewhere along the way I had lost or misplaced my clutch and my cell phone. I had to trust that Robert had taken care of my things. Trust was all I had at the time, that and a deep craving for what was going to happen.

I emptied the gift bag and took inventory of its contents. A toothbrush, a razor, douche, perfume, lotion, and nail clippers. He liked a tidy woman.

I caught a glimpse of myself in the full wall mirror and I cringed. I looked rough, tired. This was all going to be needed.

I did everything I needed to with what he gave me, then went to the shower that had filled the large room with steam by that time. I watched through the heaviness and saw my reflection in the mirror as I pulled my blouse up over my head and dropped it at my feet. My arms slithered out of my bra straps and I unhooked it from the back, holding it at my side momentarily while I looked down at my breasts. I cupped them with my hands, pushing them softly together as my libido heightened.

Stepping out of my sandals I unbuttoned my skirt from the back and let it fall as well. And there I stood with not a stitch of clothing on. I examined myself in the mirror for a moment before stepping into the warm water cascading from a large square shower head suspended from the ceiling.

It felt good running down my body. I enjoyed the soap gliding across my skin, up my arms, across my stomach, and in between my legs. My fingers slid easily between my folds increasing my arousal. My hands caressed my tits, thumbs rubbing across my nipples.

Oh God, it felt good.

I closed my eyes and ran my hands down my ass cheeks, gliding my fingers over my pussy from the back, my thumb teasing my asshole. I opened my mouth slightly, arousal swirling around me. I worked my fingers across my holes and into my folds, pushing my fingers inside me as the water ran over me. I didn't know what Robert had in store for me, but I couldn't take it any longer. I needed release.

I huffed each breath out feeling my orgasm creep closer. My fingers worked the parts that I knew would give me what I craved and when it finally washed over me I shuddered, smiling at the sweet sensation.

The towel I found was big enough to cover my whole bed back home. I wrapped myself in it and walked to a shelf on the wall. The garments Robert had picked out for me were something out of a Victoria's Secret catalog. How he came to possess such things was a question I doubted I'd have an answer for, but it excited me to know he wanted to take care of me.

I picked them up and held them out in front of me. He had good taste, simple, sexy. I opened the towel and set it on the floor and fed my legs into the black lace panties. I held the satin mini dress up to my shoulders and it only reached the top of my thighs. I pulled it over my head and let it fall into place, the straps as thin as spaghetti. It was alluring and made me feel sensual. I ran my hands over the material and watched myself as I moved in it.

There was no hairdryer that I could find so I ran my fingers through my damp hair and let it hang loose over my shoulders. It cascaded down over my breasts almost to my navel. I was almost ready.

Taking in a deeper breath I set my eyes on the blindfold he had removed. This was it. The turning point. Did I really want this? I was excited to feel him where I had only ever imagined him to be. But I was also scared to death. Robert had the ability to do whatever he wanted with me, including hurting me or worse, death. Did I trust him enough to give him total control?

I picked it up and ran it through my fingers, a tingling sensation hitting me between my legs again. I raised it to my face, and watched the image in the mirror until it was taken from me by the scarf. I wrapped it around my head and tied it tight, plunging myself back into total darkness.

I leaned against the counter feeling vulnerable and timid. I was ready, but how would he know? Should I open the door? Yell out to him? Knock on the door? Was he waiting on the other side? The door opened and I stiffened, my hands clutching the side of the counter. There had to have been a camera someplace in that bathroom. Did he watch me the whole time? I worked on controlling my breathing and calming my nerves as he approached me. I felt the heat from his body close to me. A finger ran across my mouth, pushing inside and pulling me away from the counter.

"You look beautiful, Mia." His words melted me.

He took my hand and led me out of the room, my bare feet appreciating the cool tiled floor as it changed to soft carpeting. Rose and vanilla reminded me of its existence. I tried setting up the layout of his apartment in my head with every turn we took and the smells of each room.

When he let my hand go, I stopped. Another door closed behind me and the faint smell of leather wafted around me.

My hair was pulled away from my neck and tugged back into a ponytail, his fingers trailing down the sides of my neck and down over my shoulders. They continued down my arms and intertwined with my fingers. He pressed himself against my back and kissed my neck, igniting my libido deep down inside. I bent my head to give him full access and enjoyed the sensation it gave me. A cool strap closed over my wrist and tightened around it. I brought it to my nose and inhaled the smell of leather. A similar strap tightened around my other wrist. I ran my fingers over them noticing a hook of some sort on each one. I had to have been in some sort of playroom, a red room, I think they call it.

My heartbeat increased and I found it harder to breathe than normal.

"Robert?"

His lips pressed against mine and his tongue pushed inside my mouth. He deepened his kiss and moaned from his throat, the vibrations washing over me. I raised my arms to wrap them around him, but he seized my wrists and held them between us. He led me further into the room and I heard something click into the hooks on the straps that bound my wrists.

"What was that?" I asked breathlessly.

My hands were being raised up into the air until my arms were straight above my head.

"So beautiful," he muttered. Hands covered my breasts, fingers trickled down my sides and raised the thin dress I wore until I was exposed to him. He pulled it over my head and somehow it disappeared. My panties were lowered down my legs, his hands picking each foot out of them. A strap was placed around each of my ankles and tightened firmly before my legs were cinched apart.

"Your breasts heave with each struggling ragged breath you take."

Something soft and cool raked across my chest.

"Your vulnerability is sexy." His voice broke. "Tantalizing. So fucking appetizing."

Warmth surrounded my nipple. He sucked on it hard, his tongue flicking the tip causing it to harden to a pebble.

He moaned.

I shivered.

He slid his hands up my naked sides and pressed my breasts together to indulge in both nipples.

I dropped my head back, the sensation of his actions flowing through me. Arousal began between my legs, an ache slowly spreading across my abdomen. His fingers moved down my stomach into my pubic hair and pushed into the folds of my pussy. I gasped as he moved them back and forth, his mouth still suckling my nipple. He only removed his hands for a moment but replaced them with something harder, something cold to the touch. It was large, wide but rounded. It moved back and forth across my clit, the coolness dissipating. I heard a click and the device vibrated. Arousal shot through me. I pushed my hips forward as best as I could in the position I was in. The vibration increased and my hips pushed forward further. I started humping the air like a dog in heat climbing one step closer to another orgasm. I wanted it bad.

"Yes," I whispered. A click and the vibration was gone. I panted in frustration. "Wait. No. I was so close. Please."

His body pressed against mine and his arms fed around my waist. He hugged me close, his lips nibbling on my ear. "I want you this way. Wanting. Needing. Craving. You weren't supposed to pleasure yourself in the shower, Mia."

"I knew you were watching me."

"I was. And I liked it." His voice was so close to my ear that it made me shiver when he spoke so softly but demandingly. "I would have punished you for what you did, Mia. But you were unaware of the rules. So, all I can do is push you to that cliff again. Bring you so close to exploding, then stealing it from you. I want you dangling on the edge so far that one soft blow of my mouth on your *cunt* will set you off."

I swallowed hard. His tongue trailed down my neck. He lowered himself to his knees and his hands gripped my hips. Without warning, his tongue pushed into my pussy and he lapped at my clit, the tip of his tongue teasing in just the right spot until I was panting and begging for release again. He let me go, stood back up, and kissed me with his tongue on mine forcing me to taste myself.

"It's just the beginning, my sweet." He let me go, his voice getting further away, then silence. Did he leave? Was he right in front of me, staring at my vulnerability?

My lip quivered. Something dragged down the center of my back and over my ass cheek. He made circles there before cracking it against my skin. I jumped and panted harder. It cracked again in the same spot pain searing through my cheek. The warmth of his hand rubbed me there, traveling down to my pussy and sliding a finger inside me. He moved it in and out slowly and my inner thighs were slick with my sex.

He removed his hand and slapped me with a flogger or some sort of leather whip, pain spreading across my cheek again. He rubbed it with his hand and slid down to my pussy again. This went on repeatedly several times until I welcomed the delicious mix of pain and pleasure. I was soaked between my legs and so aroused I could hardly breathe. My arms were lowered, and my legs were let go. He removed my blindfold, and I was introduced to the room for the first time. My instincts were right. It was his playroom. It was incredible. It was intimidating.

"Oh. My. Um." I walked around the room, the straps still bound to my wrists and ankles. A large X wrapped in leather was bolted to one of the black walls, several straps on each appendage. A black leather chair sat next to it with the same straps along the arms and the legs. The table along another wall reminded me of an OB-GYN appointment but matched the rest of the *furniture* bound in black leather. The wall behind me hung several vibrating devices, floggers, whips, and other scary things I had never seen in real life.

He watched me take it all in, a smile on his face and a bulge in his pants.

"Are you, um." I pointed at the wall of toys. "Are you going to use these on me?"

"I might. It depends on how I feel in the moment."

I sucked in a ragged breath and rubbed my arms, vulnerability seeping in.

"Come here." His tone was calm but still unnerving.

I walked toward him, my arms still crossed over my chest. He cupped my face and kissed me tenderly. "I have been waiting for this day for a long time since I met you."

"You have?"

He nodded, his eyes drunk with desire. He turned me around and kissed the side of my neck as his hands roamed over my arms and down my sides. He gently pushed me forward until I was against the OB-GYN-like table. He pushed against my upper back and bent me over until I rested my chest on the cool leather. He spread my legs apart, his fingers playing and pushing me toward that cliff again. I heard his belt clink together as he removed it from his pants. He fed it around my neck and held it tight as he slapped my ass cheek. When he pressed his body against my ass, I felt his cock push between my legs. He was naked and hard.

I held my breath, waiting for the moment he penetrated me, but he didn't. He slid it back and forth against my pussy, his hand slapping my ass. He spread my cheeks apart and teased my asshole before slapping my ass again.

"Fuck," I grunted, frustrated and craving for release. I pushed back against him and he stepped away from me to watch me squirm. He moved around to the front of me, seizing my wrists. He pulled them forward and locked them into place on the table before sauntering around behind me again.

I tried looking back at him, but my compromising position wouldn't allow me much mobility. Where was he? I didn't hear a door open. I couldn't hear footsteps in the heavily carpeted room. I couldn't see him or feel him. He disappeared. His hands were gone. His mouth was gone. There was no more cock to push into me. I felt desperate. Then….

Click. Vibration. I inhaled deep and closed my eyes waiting for it to press into me. A whirlwind of emotions rushed back. The moments added together and dragged on. A whimper escaped my lips. The hesitation was killing me. When the hard plastic head finally touched me, I jumped as if it wasn't expected.

He slid it back and forth only a few times before I heard it hit the floor next to my foot. It still vibrated but nothing was done about it. Soon, it was forgotten as his hands grabbed my hips and his dick pushed against my hole.

I held my breath. He penetrated me inching in, rocking back and forth, the back feeding my craving on the brink of begging him for more, the forth pushing deeper just enough to release the crazy in my mind. The huffing and panting of my breathing didn't match the pattern. That's when I realized it was Robert's broken inhales that I was hearing. He was as mentally invested in this as I was.

That, in itself, gave me a level of satisfaction I had been waiting for since the moment I stepped foot in New York. I absorbed his hands as they caressed my ass cheeks. I savored the way he fucked me, moving with awareness, sensitivity, but dominating and controlling. It wasn't just in and out. It was pushing in all of his emotion, his passion, his desire for this moment and pulling out my need for his hands on my body, his cock inside me, his control over me, his experience to finally be written in my life instead of merely in my mind.

I was being shoved dangerously close to orgasm. I was hanging off that cliff and Robert was the only thing I had left to hang on to. But, in fact, he was hanging on to me; not letting me go, not letting me fall, but teasing, dropping me close to the point of no return only to yank me back up to dangle me there again.

I squeezed my eyes closed, my mouth dry from heavy breathing. I ached all over for release. Reality was disconnecting from my mind. I tried to keep a rhythm going, with my breathing, with my body, with everything even though I wanted to scream out to him. I was fearful that he'd stop again. I was there, ready to drop off that cliff, ready for sweet release.

But, even that was ill-fated. He knew. And he stopped, withdrew and disappeared from what I knew as the only existence at the moment. My release slowly slithered away. I cried out and fought the binds around my wrists. "Let me go," I grunted.

He appeared before me and did just that. The leather cuffs were unhooked from the table and I was free. He stepped back, only his white dress shirt on, unbuttoned and dangling off his broad shoulders. His cock protruded forward, his arms hung at his sides, his face wore a melancholy frustration. He was giving me the option to leave but silently begging me to stay. Leaning against the wall, he crossed his arms over his stomach and pursed his lips. He'd never beg me to stay. He'd never ask me if I wanted to.

I didn't give him the satisfaction of an answer when I stood up off the table and pulled my legs together. I ached from the position I had been in, but I ignored it. I trembled with the need for that orgasm he dangled me close to, but I fought to suppress it.

Walking around the table, I approached him. "You're giving me an option."

He nodded and drunkenly blinked.

"Why? It's not like you to give up like this. You pursue until you conquer. It's your ammo."

"You're different. I can't let you go. You're my queen I share my experiences with."

"Queen." The title empowered me. I was no longer one of his experiences. We were a team adventuring through his sexual experiences together. I stopped in front of him, inches from his face. Looking up at him, I was ready for the next step. "Let me show you what I was looking for, what I wanted, what I crave." I slid my hands across his chest and kissed close to his nipple, my tongue running across it.

He sighed heavily, his hands feeding into my hair. He straightened up off the wall, planting his feet and preparing himself for what he knew was coming.

I lowered myself down to my knees, my arms still stretching up to his chest. They caressed his body slowly moving down and around his hips to his buttocks. I rounded my tongue and cradled the head of his cock with it. I gazed upward to watch the hunger in his eyes grow, his mouth hanging open as he watched me work. Leaning forward I opened my mouth wider, my tongue protruding as far as it would allow. His head disappeared into my mouth as my tongue cradled it, pushing it up to the roof of my mouth. I closed my lips around it and sucked on the ridge flicking his hole with my tongue.

"Oh, fuck yeah." His head hit the wall and his hands pressed me closer.

I inched him in deeper relaxing to do what I set out to do. I moved my mouth around the hard piece of meat taking a big breath and opening my throat for what I had only done one other time in my life. Moving closer, his dick hit the back of my throat and cinched past my gag reflex. It threatened me, but I closed my eyes and meditated it away before moving my face closer to his pelvis. His cock pushed past it. I raised myself up to straighten the path inward and swayed my body back and forth, my mouth rocking on his cock. Each time I took him in it was another inch deeper until he filled my throat, and his veins scrubbed the tender tissue surrounding my esophagus. His pubic hairs tickled my cheeks as I held him there and shook my head before backing off to refill my oxygen levels. I continued this form of ecstasy until I began tasting the thickness of his cum. He was close. I rocked my mouth back and forth a few more times, his ragged breathing beginning to cut out. That was my cue.

I pulled him out of my mouth and stood up, wiping my lip with the back of my hand. It took him a minute, his head still back against the wall, his panting heavy and hard. When he finally looked at me, I smiled. "Tit for tat."

I turned to walk away and finish teaching him his lesson when he lunged at me, picking me up and angrily carrying me out of the room.

"What are you doing? Where are you taking me?"

He walked heavy-footed down a long hallway and into a bedroom where he threw me on a large bed. The room was dark, very clean but with not a hint of a sexual play toy. One would never have guessed it was a bachelor pad or jiggalo's bedroom.

He tore his shirt off his arms and jumped onto the bed over the top of me. "This is what you want. I can't play games with you any longer," he grunted.

He grabbed my knees and shoved my legs apart, pushed his hands underneath my head, and covered me with his body. There was no longer hesitation. There was no room for teasing or disappearing. This was it. He bit at my lower lip while he positioned himself between my legs. His tongue pushed past my lips and filled my mouth the moment he penetrated my pussy. He grabbed my shoulders and thrust deep into me until our pubic bones rested against each other and he stopped, his tongue dancing and exploring inside my mouth. He ignited me, a fire raging across every inch of my body and he rode me with a vengeance until my fire burned out of control. I was flung over that cliff and headlong into an orgasm that grabbed hold and rattled me like a rag doll. I cried out grabbing fistfuls of blanket in my hands.

He slammed into me, grunting like a dog in heat, his hands bearing down on my shoulders and his cock quaking inside me. He drained every drop he had inside me before collapsing over the top of me in exhaustion.

The next morning, I awoke in the same bed with the sun streaming through the windows. The room seemed different. Normal. My body ached. I looked around the room. I was alone. My clutch and my phone sat on the bed stand next to me with my clothes folded neatly on the chair.

I sat up, the blanket falling away from me. "Robert?" Was I truly alone? I climbed out of the bed and pulled his dress shirt that draped over the back of the chair on my body. Buttoning the front, I quietly ventured out of the room in search of him. The hallway fed into a large living room and a bay window that overlooked the entire city. A side door opened to a balcony and a man half-naked sipping a whiskey in a short glass.

I watched him through the window for a few minutes before opening the door and joining him. "Good morning," I cooed, wrapping my arms around him from the back.

"It is, yes. How did you sleep?"

"Like a baby. You seem preoccupied, or deep in thought. Care to share?"

"No." He turned around and embraced me planting little kisses along my forehead. "But I will say you have changed me."

"Have I? For the better I hope, if that's what you need."

"It is. And you did. I want more in life. Not just pussy when I feel it benefits me. I want a woman behind that pussy. When do you have to go back?"

"Soon. Will this change things with us?"

"Never. I'll always call you out of the blue to share me with you."

I smiled and rested my head against his chest. "Hmm. I like that."

"I'm not sure what I need, but it will always include you."

~ **CHAPTER 4** ~

Married Bi-Curious Woman
Finally Explores

I stared up at the ceiling lying flat on my back, the morning sun warm on my face. The little beach house was ours for the month and the gentle lapping of the waves just outside our open bedroom window soothed me.

Marcelo had just turned off the shower and I could hear him softly singing one of his songs he had written. He was happy, and that was important to me. I rolled to my side gathering the sheets around me as I watched the crack in the bathroom door, catching the occasional glimpse of my new husband's nakedness.

He was a beautiful man, muscular, dark Italian skin, and a full head of black hair. He came from old money, a big family, and a faith in God that he loved almost as much as he loved his mother. I had it all.

I rolled to my other side and inhaled the salty air before pushing myself up to sit on the side of the bed. Burying my toes into the soft carpet I stood up and stretched, the sheets falling away from me.

The bedroom was light and airy in the daytime hours with lighting to soften and romanticize the area at night. It was the perfect rendezvous.

I shuffled across the room, pulled the balcony doors open, and walked out onto the deck. It was liberating to feel nothing but the cool morning air on my body as I enjoyed the ocean set out in front of me.

"Good morning, sexy baby." Marcelo's arms snaked around my waist and his warm body pressed against my back. I leaned my head to give him access to the side of my neck as his lips smooched against my skin. "You smell delicious this morning."

"Hmmm." I closed my eyes and smiled, feeling his hands roam up to my breasts. "Are you hungry?"

"For you, I am." His kisses pressed into my skin a little harder. "I cannot believe I get this every morning for the rest of my life."

"There is some fresh fruit from the market I left in the cabana."

"Bring in some strawberries. I'll run them along your pussy before I devour them, then devour you."

He cupped his hand under my chin and craned my head toward him, his tongue slipping through my lips and dancing around inside. He tasted minty, fresh, and he knew just how to touch me. His hands glided along my curves, reaching between my legs to cup my pussy for a moment. They wandered back up my stomach to my breasts to press them together then back down over my sides to my ass. Small arousal tickled me deep inside. He bent forward and scooped me up into his arms, his mouth on mine. His arms hooked around my legs and he lifted me off the deck and carried me down the three stairs to the beachy sand. I shivered when he lowered me onto the lounge chair facing the ocean. It could have been from his touch and the anticipation he was going to make love to me out in the open, but I was more inclined to think it was from the cool morning air.

Marcelo and I had only been together for a year before getting married. It wasn't a long time, but marriage seemed like the right thing to do. He was head-over-heels in love with me, he didn't want for anything and he treated me like a queen. His family adored me. I had everything I wanted, so why did I keep my true feelings buried so far down that even I didn't want to entertain them?

We were kissing heavily as he cradled me into the cushions of the lounge chair, keeping my legs open as he nestled himself over the top of me. His body was hard against mine and his mouth grew needy. His hands closed around my wrists and pulled them over my head pinning them to the top of the chair.

"My sexy wife," he growled, his teeth raking across my skin. "I want to buy this little beach house and live here forever with you. Make love on the beach every morning. Eat fruit and drink wine every evening. Long naked walks on the beach, swimming in the ocean. It would be incredible, don't you think?"

"Mmhmm." I kept my eyes closed as he planned one of many fantasy futures between heavy kisses.

I pulled my knees up and opened for him as I played a favorite porn scene in my head. Images of 'Kiara' going down on 'Jasmine' mixed with Marcelo's hands and lips all over me fueled my libido and pushed my arousal into overdrive.

I cooed while Marcelo slithered himself down past my navel and buried his knees into the sand, his mouth on my torso, lips smooching, tongue licking, teeth biting. I imagined long blonde hair caressing my breasts, fingernails softly scratching down to my sex. I arched my back and bent my head upward feeling fingers slide into me. It was exquisite the way they moved in and out, slowly, teasing me, drawing my arousal closer. His mouth covered me there, tongue gliding into the grooves, lips pinching lips, teeth biting what they wanted to bite. I winced at the pain, but it mixed deliciously with the pleasure pulsating within me.

Planting my feet on the edge of the chair by my ass, I thrust my hips up into the air. Marcelo moaned, bringing me out of my fantasy porn scene. His arms closed around my thighs and he held me there as he feasted, bringing me to the brink of orgasm. I pulled myself up off the chair into a full sit-up until I was sitting on his shoulders, my legs hooking around his head. He squatted in the sand, his mouth doing things to my pussy that spread a soft orgasm through me. This was always his first move during sex. He was proud that he could get me off so quickly, then he could fuck me for a long time after.

He let me down, and I dug my feet into the cool sand until he stood up and took my hand to lead me back toward the beach house. I followed him back up onto the balcony that hooked around the house to the hideaway jacuzzi the size of our master bed waiting for us back home.

He pulled the top off of it and ran his hand through the water giving me time to take him in. He was in amazing shape and I loved watching his muscles flex and move as he did. I always felt he deserved better than I could give him, but he insisted on me. He insisted on pouring all of his love and energy into my life, so I let him. It was better than living alone while I tried paying my way through art school and figuring out what I really wanted out of life. Honestly, I was as lost as one could be.

Marcelo climbed in and took my hand until I climbed the stairs, feeding my legs slowly into the heated water. It bubbled around us and tickled me until I was submerged. He sat across from me and watched me as he often did.

"I'm the luckiest man in the world, Gaia."

I forced a humble smile and shielded my eyes away from him the way I knew he liked. I did love him, just not the way he wanted me to. He always told me he'd change that.

I closed my eyes and tilted my head back to feel the sun on my face. This was nice. His hands cupped my face, and I opened my eyes to his lips brushing against mine. My mouth fell open and invited his tongue inside.

"Good morning!" A distant voice called up to us from the beach.

Marcelo grunted in frustration and pulled away a bit. His eyes set into mine, he smiled and shrugged. "We almost made it through our honeymoon without distraction."

I welcomed the rude interruption but waited for Marcelo to make the first move. He waved at two women walking toward us. I ducked out and climbed out of the tub from the other side, sneaking into the house to find coverage for us. I ran to the dresser and quickly slipped into a pair of shorts and a tank top while I looked around for something for him. His sweatpants were in a pile on the floor, so I grabbed them and walked back out in time to see them climbing the stairs. This entrapped Marcelo in the tub with not a stitch of clothing on. He shot a look at me that made me chuckle.

"Sorry for the intrusion, but my girlfriend and I had to take a walk on this glorious morning. We are renting the place just down the beach for the week." She leaned toward me and held her hand out. "I'm Jasmine."

Jasmine. I took her slender hand in mine and shook it briefly as I stole a look at her. Long dark brown hair piled high on her head and a simple strapless summer dress hugged her curves in all the right places. She had no makeup on, and her skin was flawless with a glow from the summer sun that appealed to me.

"This is Alex."

A little more on the manly side, but...strikingly beautiful. Her short blonde bob set off the features of her face, her piercing blue eyes standing out for the world to marvel at. She didn't seem much for dresses, but she sure could pull off old denim jean shorts and a white tank top.

I didn't know if it was the fact that they were a gay couple, or if it was the similar name, I was used to hearing moaning with orgasms from Kiara's mouth on her pussy, but something contracted the muscles around my vagina.

"It's good to meet you," I said softly, glancing at Alex. "I'm Gaia. This is Marcelo."

"Hiya," he called out behind me, still submerged waist-deep in the water. "How are you liking the island?"

"It's beautiful here." Jasmine leaned against the rail at the top of the stairs. "I don't think I ever want to leave."

I watched Alex. She didn't seem to want to be there like she was put out of her place. "We've been here about a month," I said, waiting for those blue eyes to look at me. She kept her head down as she twirled a gold ring around her thumb. "It is nice, but I'm starting to miss home."

"I can understand that. Paradise is paradise for a reason. I bet the locals don't feel the same about the place like we do."

The air between us grew a little thick as I struggled with conversation. Marcelo was usually the one to keep things flowing in awkward situations, but he was a little restrained at the moment.

"We don't want to keep you from anything, but we were talking and wanted to invite you to brunch later. We're pretty social people and there aren't many around. We'd love to get to know you."

"Tomorrow is our last day here, but I don't see why we couldn't." I turned toward Marcelo and smiled. "What do you think, honey?"

"I'm down for some good grub and conversation. Absolutely. It's a date."

Jasmine smiled at me, a little pink touching her cheeks. "I have to admit that we took a similar walk yesterday, earlier in the morning. We saw you here."

"We must have missed you."

"We didn't intrude because, well, you were sort of busy." She pointed toward the ocean where Marcelo and I swam during the sunrise before making love where the water crashed up onto the shore. It wasn't the most comfortable way of fucking, but it was good. The salt from the water had rubbed me in some of the wrong places and chapped my skin.

"You...saw us?" I asked, heat collecting uncomfortably between my legs.

"Don't be embarrassed. It was beautiful."

I wasn't embarrassed in the slightest. The thought turned me on. Alex turned me on. Flashes of what our new friends looked like in bed together formed in my mind. My favorite fantasy with these two. They were both slender and beautiful.

I cleared my throat and looked at Alex. "You don't talk much, do you?"

"Not really. You learn more when you stay quiet." Her smirk was sexy. Her eyes smoldered when they locked with mine. It made me feel funny inside and I think she knew that.

"A little alcohol and she doesn't stop talking," Jasmine chuckled. "We will get out of your way. Let you get back to each other." She turned to go and hesitated when she looked at Marcelo. "We are the next beach house about a mile down the beach."

"Perfect. Give us a bit and we will join you."

"We will see you in, say, a couple of hours, then? Mimosas and steamed clams on us."

"We will bring a bottle of wine," Marcelo called out.

"See you then." Jasmine laced her fingers with Alex's, and they walked away.

I didn't move from the rail, watching them until they were several feet down the beach. "What do you think their story is?"

"I don't know." Marcelo sunk back into the tub. "They seem fun though. I love gay women. Men too. They know how to live life."

"And we don't? You could have been a little more social," I teased, realizing I still had his sweatpants over my arm. I flung them in his direction, and they landed in the water. He lunged at them but ended up losing them in the bubbles. I burst out laughing when he came up with them sopping wet in his hands.

"These would have been nice five minutes ago."

"Just like that?"

"Oh, yeah? You think that's funny?"

He scrambled up the side of the tub with them in his hands and set his sights on me. I squealed, knowing what his plan was. Running into the beach house, I thought it would have been my sanctuary, but he didn't care. He ran in after me, his dripping sweatpants still in his hand.

"No, no, no, no, no," I begged, my hands reaching out toward him. He had me in a corner, his pants balled up in one hand and ready for launch. "Listen. Let's talk about this."

"Oh, *now* you want to negotiate."

I straightened up and lifted my top to expose myself to distract him. He liked it. His cock rose slowly, and I played into his desires, rubbing myself for him. Just when he started lowering his weapon, I made a run for it past him toward the back door. He lunged at me and got a hold of my waist with his free arm, tackling me to the floor, both of us laughing at ourselves.

Small kisses turned into longer ones that ended up with tongue-to-tongue contact, deepening with urgency and intense breathing that was initially interrupted by our beautiful guests.

Marcelo wrapped his hands around my wrists and held them pinned to the floor above my head. He pushed my legs apart with his and allowed his weight to settle on me. I could feel the mass of his cock through my shorts, and it set my arousal free.

"God, I love you," he mumbled between kisses. He rolled off me enough to inch my shorts down my legs and hooked them with his toes to discard them into oblivion. He positioned himself back on top of me, laced his fingers with mine, held my arms high above my head, and pushed himself inside me.

I welcomed it, the massive fill of him stretching me. He moved forward and backward slowly at first, then picked up his pace. The soft carpet underneath me was a much better bed than the sand on the beach. I moved between him and the floor, my eyes catching the open door out onto the balcony. The thrill of our new friends coming back and catching us... again... lit me on fire. My breathing got heavier. I kept my eyes on the doorway and imagined them there, touching each other while their eyes were on us.

Reaching down, I grabbed Marcelo's ample ass and pulled him into me, wrapping my legs around him and thrusting my hips in a pattern with his movements. With the thoughts in my head and his massive cock inside me, it didn't take long to feel the excitement of my second orgasm threaten to spill over me.

"Oh, baby," he whispered, his nose nuzzling into my cheek. "Yes, baby."

He was close. He huffed each time he pushed into me. I rose my hips to meet those thrusts. When he grunted, I pressed my pelvis tight into the air pressing hard into him until the friction between us pushed me over the orgasmic ledge. I held onto his hands still in mine and enjoyed the ride back down to earth.

"That," he said, breathless as he rolled off me "was spectacular."

"Agreed." I ran my hand up his chest after rolling toward him. Small kisses along his nipple made him smile. I appreciated him. He was good to me.

"I'll race you to the shower," he said, not moving from where he lay.

"At this pace, I'll be done and at the neighbor's before you are on your knees."

"I'd get down on my knees for you."

"Come on, Casanova. Let's get moving." I slapped his shoulder and climbed to my feet.

~ ~ ~ ~ ~ ~ ~ ~

After a long hot shower, we dressed simple but beachy for our date with the neighbors. Marcelo selected a vintage wine he had purchased in town and we walked along the beach until we spotted the next beach house.

Alex was on the back deck pulling clams out of their steamer when she spotted us. She disappeared in through double sliding doors momentarily and reappeared with a smiling Jasmine right behind her.

"You made it!"

"We did. And we brought wine," he said proudly, holding it up for inspection. "Do you have a bottle opener?"

"If you go inside, you'll see the kitchen on the right. You should see one right there on the counter."

"Perfect." Marcelo leaned toward me and pecked a kiss on my cheek, then carried the bottle inside.

"It's so good to see you again," Jasmine smiled. "Please, make yourself at home." She motioned toward a small table with a bamboo umbrella shielding the sun. "We need glasses," she said, spinning on her heels.

"At least we didn't forget the wine," I chuckled. "I'm sorry."

"No worries. We always come prepared." Jasmine slipped back into the house leaving me alone with Alex. I sat with my back to the ocean, watching as she came down off the deck toward me with a drink in her hand. She tipped her glass back and took a sip, looking out toward the water when she sat across from me.

The air got awkward but not entirely bad. I didn't quite understand my attraction to her, but it tugged at me each time we were close. I had a small window of opportunity to break the ice, and I took it.

"How do you like it here?" It was a bad opening line, but it was an opening line.

She shrugged, her eyes shifting to me. "It's more her thing. I'm not much for the outdoors and beachy shit."

"It's nice, I think. Good for the soul. What are you drinking? Whiskey?"

"Sazerac. It's got bourbon in it." She held her glass out toward me.

I reached across the table and wrapped my hand around it, my fingers grazing her hand. I tipped it back and let the cold liquid spread across my tongue. "It's sweet, but still burns going down."

"Exactly." She smiled playfully. "Just how I like it."

Was she flirting with me? "So, what else do you like?"

Her gaze hardened. "You really want to know?"

My muscles contracted, bringing my awareness to my sexual appetite. "I do. I wouldn't have asked if I didn't."

I held her stare and fought to maintain my composure as she shifted toward me.

"I only found three." Jasmine popped out from inside holding three wine glasses and a mug, with Marcelo following close behind her with the open bottle of wine. Alex stood up abruptly, turned back around, and went back onto the deck to tend to the clams. This was going to be a long day.

After an incredible lunch and an empty wine bottle, Jasmine broke out the mimosas. "I think it's time to celebrate."

"We really should be getting back," I said, glancing at Alex.

"But we are having so much fun." Jasmine stuck her lower lip out.

"One more won't do any harm," Marcelo insisted, his hand sliding over my knee.

"I suppose not," I smiled, sliding my glass toward them. I didn't like the way I was feeling; a little on edge, a little flirty, a little daring that grew with each sip of my drink, and extremely aroused. I concentrated on anything but Alex while they chatted about life, giggled at Marcelo's terrible jokes, and Jasmine talked about their relationship.

"Yeah," Jasmine cooed. "We met at a wedding. Neither of us was looking for love but there it was." She took Alex's hand and gazed at her, while Alex suffered through the story. Her face was flushed and the smirk on her lips divulged how much it embarrassed her.

"Alex's parents were pushing her to dance with some guy she couldn't stand just to prove she wasn't gay, so she rebelled and grabbed my hand on her way to his table. She held me close, and we danced three dances in a row, slowly, whether the song intended for a slow dance or not. We've been together ever since. That was, what?" She asked her, cocking her head inquisitively. "Two years ago?"

"Something like that," Alex mumbled, glancing up at me.

"I think that's sweet," I said. "Sometimes I wished we had that sort of story." I tried sounding completely into Marcelo, but I didn't think I had everyone convinced. "We met at a music festival. Marcelo was there playing, and I loved his music. He found me when he was finished with his set and asked me out."

"And it has been heavenly ever since," he chimed in, kissing my cheek again. "Gaia is the best thing to happen to me. I've never been happier."

I forced a smile and finished my story, my drink, and stood up. "This was really great, but we do have to get back." I took Marcelo's hand and coaxed him up out of his seat.

"She's right," he said, following me away from the table. "It was super meeting you both. If you're ever in the New York area, look us up. We are in Manhattan. Marcelo and Gaia Romano. We'd love to show you the city."

"We may just have to do that." Alex fixed her eyes on me.

"Take care, and thank you, again." I pulled Marcelo along, turning away from Alex and Jasmine with a fast-beating heart.

We walked along the beach line, my sandals in my hand, silent for the first few minutes.

"Remind me again, why we had to go so soon?"

"We have a lot to do before we leave tomorrow, and I'm not feeling all that well. I think the wine sort of went to my head."

"Aw, baby." He hooked my arm into his and rubbed it sympathetically. "When we get back, I'll draw you a nice hot bath with lots of bubbles."

"I think I just need to lie down for a little while. A nap will do me good."

"Then a nap it will be. I'll go into town and get something for dinner."

Once I was nestled in bed, Marcelo did what he promised, leaving the house with a kiss on my forehead. I heard the motorcycle start up and speed away, my eyes wide open. I whipped the covers back and climbed out of bed feeling a little woozy from the wine and not sure what to do with myself. Grabbing a beach towel, I walked down to the ocean and spread the towel over the warm sand. Stripping my dress and other garments away, I set them to the side and sprawled out on the towel. The sun was warm on my skin. My eyes closed and I thought of Alex. She was so sexy the way she moved. I caressed my stomach with my fingertips and dipped them down into my pubic hair before grazing them over my mound. My mouth fell slightly open as my fingers slid into my folds causing arousal to stir. I slid my legs open and slowly circled my clit as the sun baked me. The ocean lapped at the edge of the sand as I imagined Alex's tongue lapping at my pussy. My breathing became ragged. My hips moved up and down. My finger circled faster. My arousal pushed me to the edge, and I came hard. My back arched up off the towel as I enjoyed waves of pleasure wash over me.

Getting up, I looked around me, not a soul in sight. I peered down the beach toward their beach house about a mile down, wondering if she had thought about me in the same way. I ran into the ocean splashing the cool water all over until I was in too deep to run anymore. I dove under and swam, savoring the feel of the water against my naked body.

~ ~ ~ ~ ~ ~ ~ ~ ~

New York seemed busier than usual. It was probably the time we had spent away in a serenity that not even the birds knew how to rush by. I missed home, but I also missed the beauty of the beach. Once we got settled back into our apartment, I arranged for a cleaning company to stop by, caught up on emails, and began planning our next party.

Marcelo came out of the bedroom dressed in a nice dress shirt and his best pants.

"No," I pleaded. "You're going to work?"

"I have to."

"Actually, you don't."

He kissed the top of my head and grabbed a grapefruit on the way to the door. "I have a meeting with a record company. They are interested in my music. I can't pass this up."

"You didn't tell me."

"I did. You have been distracted."

I pursed my lips. He may have been right. "Sorry."

He opened the door and winked at me.

"Good luck," I called out as the door was closing behind him.

I let out a long sigh and looked around the apartment. I needed some action. Grabbing my purse, I hit Bryn's number and put her on speaker as I walked out the door.

"What are you doing?" I asked before she had the chance to say hello.

"Are you home?"

I nodded, "I am. Marcelo has a meeting with some record company, and I'm bored to death. Let's meet."

"You got it, girl. Coffee Project?"

"Something stronger."

"Let's meet at Bemelmans."

I bit my lower lip and smiled. "How about Stonewall?"

"Feeling daring, are we?"

"I just want to go someplace a little different."

"That is definitely different. You sure?"

"Yep."

"Okay, then. I'm on my way."

"Call Viv. I'll meet you there."

I hailed a taxi and within twenty minutes I was standing outside of the small bar. There were rows of gay pride flags hanging above it in protest of the happenings in

New York a few weeks ago. It was something political, nothing of interest to me.

Walking inside, I felt a sense of freedom as if I were part of the community there and I was finally in a safe place. Bryn and Vivian weren't there yet so I bellied up to the bar and waited for the bartender.

"Hey," she said, her eyes lighting up when she looked at me. "You're a new face."

"Yeah, hi. I don't think I've ever been in here."

"Well, have a seat and enjoy. What can I get for you, sweetie?"

"I'll take a Sazerac?"

"One sweet bourbon for the pretty lady, coming up."

Looking around the darkened bar, I noticed a couple of women sitting at a table. They were holding hands over the table and seemed to be deep in conversation. The larger woman sporting tattoos up her arms and a large leather vest reached across and moved a strand of the skinny girl's hair out of her face. She tucked it behind her ear before returning her hand to the other three.

Another couple sitting on a window seat was doing everything but talking. One sat on the other's lap with her tongue so deep in her lover's mouth she was tickling her tonsils. One hand was up her shirt and the other one was fondling her ass cheek.

"Don't pay any attention to them," the bartender interrupted. "They are always in here doing that."

"Have they ever…?"

"Had sex here? No. I won't let it get that far. They live upstairs in one of the apartments up there and this is their excitement, I suppose."

"They seem happy."

"I guess. They have only been together a few months."

I took a sip of my drink feeling that familiar burn down to my stomach as I watched them. My face must have exposed how much I truly appreciated the mix of bourbon and slightly sweet liqueur.

"That good, huh?" the bartender chuckled.

"I'm… trying new things," I shrugged.

"So, what about you? You with anyone?"

If I told her I was straight, would she force me to leave? "I'm waiting for some friends. They are supposed to meet me here."

"Girlfriends?"

"Um, no. I don't have a girlfriend right now." I didn't lie.

"That's too bad," she smiled. "This one is on me." She tapped the top of the bar next to my drink.

I opened my mouth to say something, but thought better of it, deciding to enjoy the attention. It was why I was there after all, right?

The front door opened, and Bryn and Vivian walked in, Viv b-lining it directly toward me.

"Hey, guys," I smiled, hugging each one.

"Why did you choose *this* place?" Viv's eyes were wide, and she acted nervous.

"Why not? It's a little different, fun, could be exciting."

"People *died* out front a few weeks ago," she whispered.

"That's fake news," the bartender said, walking back to our side of the bar. "No one died. Promise." She dragged her finger over her heart in an x.

Vivian exhaled a big breath and mellowed out. She tended to be a little more dramatic more naive than she needed to be, but she had a sweet heart.

"What can I get for you?"

"Do you have White Claw?" Vivian asked curiously.

"I do. Lemon, watermelon, or black cherry?"

"Lemon, please?"

"I'll just take a glass of Merlot," chimed Bryn. "Let's grab a table."

After they got their drinks we sat at a table near the back, and I observed everyone around me. There weren't many there at the time, but as the day wore on it filled up with others.

Music played and the alcohol flowed nicely. I was getting used to the bourbon taste, but it was hitting me a little harder than I was used to, so I alternated a sip or two for water. Vivian danced with a woman she had met in the bathroom and seemingly couldn't detach from her. She pulled the woman to our table with excitement in her voice.

"You guys. You have to meet my new friend. Her name is Sasha. She is a talent scout from 42nd Studios and she is looking for some new girls." She leaned in, her eyes widening. "She said I was funny and there was something about me."

"It's good to meet you," I said, jetting my hand out toward the long slender woman. I shot Viv a 'be careful' look.

"Likewise. Your friend has a good chance at getting in with our agency. She has that certain something we are looking for right now. If she can act, she may just have what it takes."

"She's good," I confirmed. "Would you like to join us?"

"For a minute. I'm supposed to be meeting my girlfriend for dinner. She's late, as usual." She pulled a chair out and sat down, Vivian pushed a chair closer to her to sit as close as possible without being on the woman's lap. "Ah, there she is."

I heard the door behind me and watched as Sasha waved her hand in the air. She smiled, stood up, and slid her arm around the woman's waist.

"You're late," she said to the short-haired blonde woman.

"I'll make it up to you later." They locked lips and intimacy swirled around them.

I was entranced. She reminded me so much of Alex that my body instantly responded. Same haircut, same persona, same stance. It was uncanny.

"I'm sorry," Sasha pulled back a bit and smiled. "This is my girlfriend, Reese."

Vivian stood up, a slight pout on her lips. "I'm Vivian. This is Bryn and Gaia."

"Nice to meet you all," she said with a passive caution.

I couldn't stop staring at her. And I didn't until my phone buzzed. Marcelo texted me that he was home and had some amazing news, but he wanted to tell me in person. I hesitated to answer as I looked back up at Reese. Uncanny.

She leaned into Sasha and whispered something in her ear, seemingly a little on edge about being there. Sasha reached for her purse and I perked up. "Would you like to join us for a drink?" I spat. "I was just about to buy the next round."

"Just one," Sasha pleaded.

Reese nodded and sat down. The bartender noticed and came to our aid. We ordered, received, drank, and that round fed into others.

I picked up my phone and sent Marcelo a text.

Out with the girls. Sorry I didn't respond earlier. Will see you later tonight?

I set my phone back onto the table and gave Reese my attention as her girlfriend unraveled an epic story about one of Reese's embarrassing moments. It was obvious Reese wasn't pleased that she was being exposed in this way, but it didn't stop Sasha from telling it.

I wondered if all gay couples went through such torture. Jasmine couldn't wait to tell similar *epic* stories about Alex, even though it was evident she didn't want her to. And now, this.

I wanted to rescue her. The moment she looked at me I stood up. "Excuse me for a moment. Time to find the little girls' room." I left my things on the table and walked toward the bathroom.

"Hold up." Reese pushed her chair away from the table and joined me. "I'll come with."

We walked in silence to the back corner of the bar until we were in the bathroom.

"Your girlfriend seems nice."

"She's got to go." She leaned on the sink and looked at her face in the mirror. Her short blonde hair was spiked on the top. She wore a little lip gloss but nothing more. A tattoo sleeve wound down around her arm sporting skulls and a horrid-looking witch riding on her broom over the top of them all.

"You don't like her?"

"I do. But she's too much."

"How long have you been together?"

"A year."

"I guess it's better to find out now before commitment happens."

"I guess. What about you? Which one is yours?"

"I'm... um.... Neither of them. We are all just friends."

She nodded and stood straight. She watched me through the mirror.

"I'm married, actually," I continued. "Newlywed."

"A guy?"

"How'd you know?"

"Sixth sense. Thanks for the distraction."

"No worries. I'm sort of on one tonight, myself."

"Newlywed and you already need a distraction? Interesting."

"Not really. I guess I'm just used to doing things my way. But I can't be single forever. He's good to me. He's got a good family."

"That's important, I guess if that's what you want in life."

"You remind me of someone I met in Bali."

"Do I?"

"Her name is Alex. She and her girlfriend rented a beach house close to ours. The sad part was we all met the day before our honeymoon was over. Was probably for the best though."

She continued watching me in the mirror without saying a word.

"Sometimes I think I talk too much." I went into a stall to pee while her words played on my mind.

"I'll see you out there," she said, the door opening.

I didn't respond. "I'm an idiot."

Anyway, Marcelo deserved better. I wasn't going to hurt him.

When I went back and joined our table, Sasha was still talking about her story, giggling, and leaning into Reese as much as Reese hated that. I sat down and picked up my phone, opening a new text from Marcelo.

Where are you? Maybe I'll meet you out. Xxx

I slid my fingertips along the side of my phone before responding.

I'm leaving soon anyway. Will see you back at the apartment.

I finished my drink and stood up. "I have to get back."

"Aw, you should stay." Bryn pulled at my arm.

"Yeah, don't be a party pooper now." Vivian chimed in.

"Marcelo is home, and he has some big news. I can't keep him waiting."

Reese smirked and I despised her for wearing her thoughts like that.

"It was really good meeting you," Sasha smiled, holding her hand out toward me. "Maybe we can get together again, sometime. This was fun."

I shook her hand and glanced at Reese. "I'd like that. It was nice meeting you both." I stood up, directing my attention to Bryn and Vivian. "I'll see you both later?"

"Are you good?"

"Yes. No, stay. Have fun. Talk soon." I got out of there before I changed my mind and hailed a taxi on the street.

~ ~ ~ ~ ~ ~ ~ ~ ~

Marcelo was in bed watching television when I got in, his bare chest exposed from the blankets around his waist. "How was your evening?"

"Okay. We met up at Stonewall in West Village."

"That gay bar?"

"Mmhmm." I pulled my shirt off as I went into the bathroom.

"Why would you go there? It's a dive bar."

"Not at all. It was actually sort of fun. Something different."

"You always did like new things."

I turned on the water to the shower drowning out Marcelo's words. Stripping down the rest of the way, I went back into the bedroom to grab my nightshirt and Marcelo pounced playfully out of the bed toward me. He slithered up behind me and wrapped his arms around my waist. "So, did you get hit on by any pretty ladies? Do I have to beat a chick up?"

"No," I giggled, fighting him off. "I have to shower."

"Yes, you do. You smell like a whiskey barrel."

I went into the steam-filled bathroom and climbed into the shower where he joined me only moments later. Warm water ran over me raising goosebumps on my skin.

"You're so sexy," he whispered from behind me. His hand glided up my side while his other hand scooped up my soap and ran it across my stomach. With his mouth on my neck and his hands slipping across my skin my arousal awoke. He lathered the soap into his hands, set it down, and thoroughly cleansed me. I raised my hands to the wall above my head and closed my eyes to savor it.

His hands moved across my breasts and down my stomach. He pushed his hands between my legs and slipped them into my folds, working their magic to heighten my arousal. The water washed the soap away but did nothing for the exhilaration swirling around my insides. He grabbed my hips and turned me toward him, lowered to his knees, and lifted my leg to the side of the tub. I grabbed hold of the top of the shower door and held my breath. His tongue pushed inside me causing adrenaline to fly through my veins.

"Yes," I whispered. I closed my eyes, dropped my head back, and opened myself to him. Alex's face flashed in my head and I imagined it was her on her knees in front of me. Her tongue lapped at my pussy. Her hands were on my thighs pushing me apart to get deeper. When she looked up at me, it was Reese. I gripped the door harder, the tip of her hard tongue running over my clit repeatedly. My breathing was hard, ragged, heavy, and orgasm seized me. I shook, as he wrapped his arms around my waist and kept me there until it subsided.

He slammed the water off and climbed out, picking me up in his arms and carrying me to the bed. Our soaked bodies clung to the blanket as he pushed my legs open, settled his weight on top of me, and entered me. He fucked me hard and fast with no build-up to it.

My orgasm returned and threatened to take over again, working its way up, building slowly with pressure. He held my wrists to the bed, thrusting into me over and over again, grunting as he did it. I wrapped my legs around him only to feel him push them away. He pulled off me, grabbed my hips, and spun me around to my knees. I dropped down onto my hands with my ass toward him and lowered my head to the mattress. His hands caressed my ass cheeks as he pushed into me and fucked me from behind. His groin slapped my cheeks with each push into me, his movements getting more intense. He slammed into me with a guttural groan from deep in his throat. His hands gripped my hips and he held me there. I could feel his cock pulsate inside me as he jerked several times.

I circled my clit a few more times with the tip of my finger until another orgasm filled me. He fell onto the bed with a smile on his face so wide it made me chuckle.

"Now we have to change the bed."

"I'll buy you a new one," he cooed.

I laid my head on his arm and grazed my fingertips across his chest. "So, what's your big news?"

"Remember that record company I met with today?"

I nodded.

"They are very interested. They want to sign me and start recording next week."

"That's great news."

"I have to fly down to Nashville for a few days and meet with some other people, but they love me."

"Nashville? What are you doing, going country?"

"I guess there is a market in the country genre for some of my music, but it's only a small part of it."

"A few days?"

"Four, tops. Do you want to come with?"

I hesitated, not because I needed to think about it. I didn't want to go. I was looking forward to some alone time, but I didn't want it to be too obvious. "I think I'll stay back. Do some planning for the party and maybe start a project of my own."

He kissed the top of my head, climbing off the bed and disappearing into the bathroom. "I need to leave in the morning. Is that okay?" The shower fired back up.

"Yes." The blanket had a large wet spot in the middle from where we were and I climbed off, pulling the blanket back. The sheets were still dry, so I went to the closet and fished another blanket out to make the bed. By the time I was finished, a clean Marcelo was walking in with a towel around his waist. He really was beautiful. He planted a kiss on my lips before losing the towel and climbing into bed. I took a quick shower myself before joining him.

The next morning, by the time I awoke, Marcelo was up, dressed, and ready for his trip. He walked in with half of a bagel in his mouth and a plane ticket in his hand. He took the bagel out with his other hand and leaned over me. "I didn't mean to wake you, but I do have to go. My flight leaves in two hours."

I nodded, pecked his cheek, and lay back down into the pillow. "Do you need anything before you go?"

"Only if you can fit inside one of my suitcases."

I smiled at how much he loved me. "When will you be back?"

"Hopefully by Thursday, but I'll let you know."

"Have a good flight. Let me know how things go."

"Will do. Kisses. Love you." He kissed his finger and blew it toward me before disappearing out of the room.

I heard his footsteps fade to the front door. The door closed and I was alone.

I walked around the apartment without a stitch of clothing on. It felt liberating. The smell of Marcelo's bagel still hinted in the air, so I grabbed one and pushed it down into the toaster. I went to the front window and pulled back the curtain to feel the sun on my skin. The people on the street were smaller than ants and the cars looked like little matchbox cars I used to play with as a child. I stayed there, leaning against the windowsill until my bagel popped up.

The rest of my morning was much like that. I talked with Vivian and found out her new connection with Sasha was a hit. She had an interview with them later in the day followed by drinks at Soho House with Sasha and a couple of others from the company. And yes, Reese was going to be there. I hinted about not having much to do since Marcelo was away and she invited me along.

I spent the rest of the day getting ready. It was more time than I had spent on my wardrobe and makeup since the day I met Marcelo. It also made me realize how badly I needed to update my closet. After finally settling on a short black sequin skirt and a white chiffon blouse that accentuated my black bra underneath, I found a pair of red three-inch heels matching my lipstick that set it off perfectly. I was probably overdressed but my excuse was an interview with an antique dealer to showcase some of my art.

The question never came up on why I had dressed so well for *just drinks.* By the time I had gotten to Soho

House, Reese was leaning against the building outside. She looked a little pissed that I had taken so long.

"Hi," I said simply, stopping in front of her.

"It's about time." She dragged her eyes down my body and back up, connecting with my eyes.

"I didn't ask you to wait outside for me."

"I sort of got elected. Invite only here. If you're not a member you have to blow someone to get in. Just so happens...."

She didn't finish her sentence. Was she implying that she expected me to drop to my knees for her?

I would have.

She pulled the front door open and showed her card. "We are with the Rousche party."

"Go right into the Champagne room. Welcome."

I nodded at the maître d and followed Reese through the main dining room into a more private area. We walked in, but no one noticed we existed, so we leaned against the wall and waited for a moment to make ourselves known.

"This the first time you've been in here?" she asked.

"Yes. Honestly, I didn't even know about this place."

"Sasha has a lot of pull here. She likes to wine and dine most of her clients here. Makes her feel sophisticated, successful."

"I get it. Appearance is eighty percent of it."

"You'd fit right in," she said, eyeing me again.

"I don't usually dress like this." I thought about using the lie I had fabricated but I had a feeling she would have seen right through it.

"You look good."

My stomach knotted. "Thanks."

Reese tried to get Sasha's attention, but she was too busy with the others in her party. Vivian sat close to her and laughed at everything the woman said. That pretty much kept me out of the loop, too.

"Come on," Reese said, leaving the room. She seemed annoyed over anything else.

I followed her out and we found two stools at the end of the bar.

"They will never notice we are gone. What are you drinking?"

"Whatever you're having is fine." I watched her as she pulled a card from her pocket and set it in front of her. The bartender noticed and walked toward us. "Two maple whiskey lemonades please." The bartender nodded and walked away. Reese kept her eyes forward and twirled her thumbs around each other. "I don't know why she talked me into coming here today."

"She likes you near her. Maybe she feels more supported, even though she isn't paying attention to you. Just the idea that you're here…."

"We broke up this morning."

"Oh. I'm sorry."

She shook her head. "Like I told you last night, it has been a long time coming. I spent most of my day moving out of her place. She practically begged me to come with her tonight. Anyway, why are *you* here?" She turned toward me.

"Same thing. I came to support Vivian, even though she doesn't know I'm alive right now."

"You ever hook up with her?"

"Viv?" There was a little more shock in my voice than intended. "No. We are friends. That's all."

"Have you… ever? Hooked up with another girl?"

Her attention was dead on me, and her question struck me hard. How should I have interpreted that? Was she asking for future reference? Small talk? Did I detect sarcasm there? "That's a little personal, isn't it?"

"It is. And your avoidance in answering tells me a lot."

"And what is that? What does it tell you?"

"You're married, unhappily, but you feel obligated. You are interested in girls like me because we can treat you the way you want to be treated and pleasure you the way you crave to be pleasured, but you're scared to try."

Heat rose up into my face. "You have it all worked out in your head, I see."

"I don't think you've really been with a woman even though you may have dabbled in college. Your man comes along and treats you right and you make hasty decisions that tell you that you should be with him because it's the right thing to do. Now, you feel stuck." She leaned into me, her fingertips grazing my knee. "Am I close?"

Her touch tightened my muscles around my vagina and knotted my stomach tighter. "I have to go." I didn't move at first. Neither did she. When I finally climbed off the barstool she stayed. "Thank you for the drink."

She nodded and watched me until I turned away and walked out the door. I kept my composure until I was out the door and back on the street. I leaned against the next building, breathless and wanting. The night sky hinted around the city lights, but it was still early, and I did not want to go back home. I pulled my cell and called Bryn, but it went to her voicemail.

"Damn it." I hung up without leaving a message. Pushing off the building, I started down the street when a hand wrapped around my arm. I tried jerking away from whoever it was until I saw Reese there.

"I'm not playing games with you." She pushed me back up against the building.

I stared wide-eyed into her face. "What are you doing?"

"I want you, Gaia. And I know you want me, too. Why are we fighting this?"

She pinned her body up against me and pressed her lips into mine. My insides caught fire as she deepened the kiss. Her tongue played around with mine, a delicious hint of whiskey and lemon taunting my taste buds. Her hand ran up my chest and wrapped around my neck, holding me there as her other hand found my thigh. It inched to the inside and up underneath my skirt.

"You're so fucking wet," she whispered. "I knew you were hot for me."

She pulled my skirt up enough to cup my ass cheek pushing herself into me harder. She was sending bolts of sensation through me from every angle, and I didn't want any of it to stop. Her hand went between my legs and I let it, opening for her. My panties were pulled to the side and when she slid her fingers deeper, I wanted to lose it. I fed my hands up in between us, her breasts tight against her chest but still full in my hands. I wanted to touch them bare. I wanted my tongue on her nipples. I wanted to taste her. It was the only thing on my mind.

"Take me to your apartment." She pulled back, her eyes devouring me. I nodded, swallowing hard.

Everything I did from hailing a taxi, waiting for it, and climbing into the back was on the back burner of my mind. All I could think about was sex... with Reese... a woman. I was soaked.

She held my hand in the cab, her thumb pressing into the soft area between my fingers. She pulled my hand to her mouth and picked up my forefinger with her tongue. She inserted it slowly into her mouth, her tongue swirling around it and gently sucking it. I couldn't take my eyes off her mouth.

She slid her other hand up my thigh to my pussy and rubbed me through my panties, pulling her hand back and replacing my finger in her mouth with her own. She closed her eyes and tasted me. My breath caught. My pussy tightened. My heart raced. Was this really happening? I could hear my own breathing in my ears.

When we pulled up in front of my apartment, my legs felt too heavy to get out of the cab. Someplace in the back of my mind, I knew this was wrong, but I kept it shoved in the darkest place I could. If I didn't think about it, it was a problem I'd have to deal with later, right?

Reese climbed out of the cab after paying him. She took my hand and pulled me along until we were in front of my door. She fed her hands around my neck to the back and grabbed handfuls of my hair. She pulled me to her and kissed me the way I craved to be kissed, with her tongue, her teeth, her lips, and her soul. She fueled me.

I fumbled with the lock on the door, finally opening it. Hands on breasts, mouths on bare skin, hips pressing together. I couldn't get enough of her.

We stumbled and fell against the wall as she tried pulling my blouse off over my head. I unbuttoned the first few buttons and that gave her a better opportunity. She stripped me of it, yanked my bra down below my breasts, and bent down with her mouth. She sucked my nipple into her mouth and toyed with it until I could feel it in my pussy. I reached for her jacket and peeled it off her arms, grabbing at her pants. I felt clumsy, unsure of what to do, but crazily insane to get it.

She helped me out of my skirt then stood back and took a big breath. Her gaze shifted from one eye to another as she tried to read my thoughts. I was all naked except for my underwear and she had her pants undone looking hot as hell.

She held her hand out and waited for me to slide my hand in hers before she led me through my own living room to our bedroom. She sat on the edge of the bed. I sat next to her. Her hand ran up the inside of my thigh, slowly, delicately, softly. Her mouth was on my shoulder. Light kisses. Soft kisses. Her hand moved upward. She touched my pussy. My breath caught. I opened my legs. She slid her hand back and forth and I lay back. She joined me for a moment, then crawled down until her face hovered over my mound. I felt dizzy from breathing so hard. She tasted me a little, but it sent a sensation bigger than I had ever felt through me. She looked up at me and smiled, then tasted again. My chest heaved up and down with each breath I took. Her tongue pushed into me and her fingers were moving around in a way that brought my arousal to a very fast head then stopped and teased the hell out of me.

"Oh, God!" I shoved my fingers into her hair and pushed her into me, begging for release. She slammed my hands away and caressed my hips as her mouth sent me into oblivion. I thrust my hips up and down, sensations flooding me and drowning me in libidinous.

She sat up and watched my body writhe in ecstasy as it slowly dissipated. She stood up and lowered her pants, then her underwear. She wore a strap-on penis and caressed it with her hand.

"Does it turn you off?" she asked, staring into me.

I shook my head. "No."

I spread my legs and hungrily watched her crawl back up onto the bed over the top of me. Her face paralleled mine. Her lips kissed mine. Her tongue traced them. Her penis slid between my folds and inched inside me. Her hands buried themselves underneath my ass and she held on tight before she started fucking me.

I could barely hold on as my arousal swirled around me pushing my orgasm to a point where I couldn't think straight. I met her hips with each thrust into me feeling her lips on my neck as she pulled my orgasm out and held me there until it was done grabbing a hold of me.

She removed the strap-on and pushed her fingers inside herself, pumping her hand in and out aggressively. I stopped her, rolled her to her back, and moved my mouth down to unfamiliar territory. I touched her there, pulling her lips apart and exploring her. Her clit was large and swollen, glistening from her own juices. I licked her there and she jumped. I twirled my tongue around it, flicking over the top several times. She grabbed the blanket underneath her and tightened her fists, her back arching and her head going back into the pillow. I moved my tongue like a figure eight around the outside of her as I slid my finger into her. I hooked my finger and found her g-spot, stroking it until she yelled out and started gyrating her hips up and down. When she collapsed, I crawled back up to her and lay next to her side. I watched her in awe. She was incredible.

The bedroom door opened, and Marcelo stood in the doorway. My heart stopped. "Marcelo!"

There was no way to cover this up. Two women lying naked with each other, breathing heavily, their pussies glistening with their juices.

I jumped up and grabbed my robe, wrapping it around me. Reese snuck off to the bathroom leaving us alone.

He slowly walked up to me and I expected his hand across my face, but he did nothing at first. His hands fed up underneath my chin and around my neck, cradling my face in his hands.

I swallowed hard. "I'm sorry." My tongue stuck to the roof of my mouth.

"Don't be." His kiss was hard, fiery, passionate, and intense. His tongue urgently searched my mouth for traces of her.

I pulled away, completely confused.

"Gaia, this is what I've been waiting for. It's why I introduced you to Alex and Jasmine. I prayed that something would happen with them, but you were so damned worried about what I would think that you suppressed everything you desired to make me happy."

"You're kidding, right? You're okay with this?" I pushed away from him and almost felt angry. "Why didn't you say anything?"

"I did. Several times. But you'd shut me out, or you'd think I was just saying that to make you happy. I don't know, but I'm glad it finally happened. I knew if I stayed away long enough someone would tempt you enough."

Reese reappeared completely dressed and smiling.

"Did you know about this?" I pointed at her with an accusing finger.

"Not completely? But I was told enough to pursue you. I'm not disappointed. I hope you're not either."

All I could do was shake my head in disbelief. But one thing I did realize that night was how much I was in love with Marcelo. He always told me he knew I wasn't, but he'd change it. And he did.

~ **CHAPTER 5** ~

Sex Games and Oral Orgasm - The Game

"How do you break down a complex mental process into something more understood? By dividing the process into smaller parts making them easier to modify and understand in part, thus creating a better understanding of the whole." I glanced at my door trying to ignore the giggles in the other room. Focusing back on my thesis, I continued reading. "Using two factors X and Y such that part Q is influenced by X but invariant with respect to Y, while part R is influenced by Y but invariant with respect to X. Given that these modules are functionally distinct…." I sighed as the giggling continued. Reaching toward my stereo, I flipped it on and turned it up enough to drown out my suitemates. "Continuing. If we are given pure measures such as FA and GR, each reflecting only part, we must prove that FA is influenced by X but not Y, while GR is influenced by Y but not X."

"You've got to be kidding me?" squealed a female voice from the other room. "That's so cute!"

I slammed my pencil down and growled at the door. Grabbing my water bottle, I opened my door and walked out with the excuse that I needed more water before continuing my thesis. I filled the bottle at the kitchen sink before poking my head into the living room.

Two half-dressed girls were bouncing around in their underwear on the couch cushions that were strewn across the floor.

"What are you guys doing?" I was irritated, but my tone did not portray that. In fact, it never did. I was always the easy-going one, but it didn't matter. "Claire. Stacy, come on. I'm trying to study."

Claire grabbed a small pillow and threw it in my direction. "Lauren, for God's sake. It's Friday. Take a pill, will ya?"

"And what would that accomplish? My thesis is due in less than a month. If I don't work steadily on it, I will not be finished in time."

Claire shot Stacy a look and I knew what it meant, but I didn't care. After this year was over, I would more than likely never see them again. Hell, I wouldn't be surprised if they never returned to campus. They were both borderline failing out of their classes. They were more concerned about the parties they attended and what they were wearing than passing their classes. I only needed the sleeping quarters. What they did with their time was none of my concern.

"Come here, Lauren." Stacy's face softened and she extended her hand to me. "Just for a minute."

I hesitated, but did as she asked, stepping over a cushion to join them on the empty couch. "What is it?"

"We have been roomies for a year and a half, and we both know how important your classes are to you. You're smart and you're going to be so successful in your neuro…psychiatry field."

"Neuropsychology," I corrected.

"Whatever." She waved her hand in the air. "The point is, you're *only* going to be successful in… that field."

"I don't understand what you mean."

"Lauren." Claire put her arm around me. "You have no social life. No fun. No sex. Nothing."

"I've had… sex before."

"That one time in your high school boyfriend's room doesn't count."

"It was more than once," I defended. "Besides, it's none of your business what I do. I need to…."

"Have fun. You need to have fun," Claire interrupted.

"No, I need to focus. My schedule is full, and I don't even know what I want to do with my life."

"We aren't trying to butt into your life, Lauren. We care about you. That's all."

"Yeah. We want to see you have some fun. Even if you don't go to a party and drink too much until you throw up. There are other things you can do besides shoving your face in your books all the time."

"Yes!" Claire jumped up. "You could go to the Collegiate Café and people watch, assess their brains, and figure them out."

"Find a hot guy and flirt obsessively with him until he's easily readable."

"Or, come out with us to a party and drink so much you puke."

I looked from Claire to Stacy and then back again. I smiled a big smile, then patted their knees with my hand. "I appreciate the gesture and the offers, but I think I'm okay. People watching is not really my thing, and as for the *hot guys* around here, I would rather watch paint dry. If there is any brawn, there is no brain."

"Who says he has to put a sentence together?" Stacy cocked her head. "Just flirt with him then fuck him. It's easy."

"You're easy," poked Claire.

"If you don't mind," I said, standing up. "I'm going to get back to my thesis. I don't intend on allowing *college life* to interfere with what's important in real life."

I walked back across the room but before I was able to get behind my bedroom door, Claire bit at me with her words.

"Work isn't everything, Lauren. You need to balance your life better or you're going to die old and alone."

"Whatever, Claire," I mumbled, taking a few more steps. I turned back toward her and crossed my arms. "For your information, I do not make this decision lightly. I have witnessed what *fun and recreation* can do to someone. I think I'm all set."

Claire erased her expression from her face and lowered her eyes to the floor. "I didn't mean…."

"I know you didn't. I'm sure you have all good intentions. But if you continue to go down the path you're trying to get me to go down…." Say it, Lauren. *You'll end up like my sister.*

I couldn't say it. Watching Kat destroy her life was the hardest thing I'd ever gone through. "Ugh, never mind." I pushed my door open and closed it quietly behind me. I bit back the tears and took a big breath.

It took me a bit to get back into the breakdown of a complex mental process, but I shook all bad thoughts from my mind and sat down. Eventually, my determination persevered.

"If we are given pure measures such as FA and GR, each reflecting only part, we must prove that FA is influenced by X but not Y, while GR is influenced by Y but not X."

I glanced up at my door when the giggling began again. I had never met anyone who liked to flirt and play around more than Claire and Stacy. They loved to flirt with everyone they encountered, and when they weren't around others, they played around with each other.

Exhaling a big sigh, I closed my books, stacked them on top of each other, and shoved them into my bag. I pulled my sweater on and walked back into the living room expecting another lesson on life. But what I witnessed was more intimacy between them than wanting to inform me of how horrible my social life was.

I tried to be as quiet as I could to avoid conversation, but just before my hand reached the doorknob, Claire stopped me.

"Where are you going? Oh, wait. Let me guess. The library?"

"I have some research to do," I lied, still trying to be the easy-going one. No confrontation was my motto.

"Research." Her tone was dead but easily readable.

"I won't be late." I opened the door without looking back.

"We will be," Stacy giggled. "It's Friday night. I'm not staying in."

I closed the door behind me and sighed, leaning against it.

Claire's words muffled through the door. "At least she's going *somewhere*. It's better than being holed up in her room."

"Come here." Stacy's voice softened and I heard the smooching of passionate kisses.

I didn't know why, but I stayed there. I listened. I eavesdropped. I was intrigued. I knew why I stayed there. I cracked open the door and watched them.

Claire's delicate fingertips ran across Stacy's breasts, through her top, and Stacy liked it. She dropped her head back, a moan escaping her lips. I gasped. She straightened her head and fed her hand into Claire's long black hair until their lips locked.

I stared, my lips parting slightly.

Stacy's tongue jetted out and teased Claire's lower lip then disappeared into Claire's mouth. Another moan wafted across the room to my ears. Who's was it? My mouth fell open, the tip of my tongue tracing my own lips. I reached up and cupped my breast as my attention got lost in their intimate scene.

Why was I so afraid of intimacy? Claire lowered her hand to Stacy's panties and wiggled them underneath the waistband. It disappeared behind the thin fabric and a moment later Stacy gasped, her head falling back.

"Yes," she cooed. "Oh, right there."

Footsteps echoing up the stairs around the corner interrupted my desire to watch and I straightened quickly, closing the door quietly. Forcing a smile just in time I nodded at the familiar girl who lived upstairs as she passed me in the hallway. Before I rounded the corner to the stairway, I glanced back at our front door, a tease of jealousy threatening me.

"Stupid," I mumbled, pushing the outside door open to the street.

The library was quiet, empty, haunting. I found a corner table and sat down for the next couple of hours where I absorbed myself into neurocognitive processes and experimental and clinical neuropsychology. Before I knew it, I was being asked to leave for closing which meant it was eleven.

If I knew my suitemates, they would have already left for some frat party or basement get-together by that time. I walked to the coffee shop and grabbed a coffee before getting back to the suite. There were still a couple of good hours in me before bed.

When I reached the suite, I heard noises inside.

"Oh, please no." I closed my eyes and hoped they had left the television on before going out. When I opened the door, Claire and Stacy were still on the couch, their faces lighting up the moment they saw me.

"Lauren! You're back." Claire jumped up and set her wine glass down before bounding toward me. Stacy followed suit.

I backed up to the door defensive to their actions. "What's going on? Why are you guys still here?"

"We have made some decisions. We need to talk to you."

"I figured you'd have gone to some party or something by now."

"Well, some things are more important than that." Claire took my hand and led me across to the couch. "Sit."

"I'm kind of tired."

"It's not a question, Lauren," she insisted.

Stacy popped in. "Yeah. It's an intervention."

"An... intervention," I repeated, my eyebrows raising.

Claire pulled me to the couch and sat down, pulling me down next to her. "Listen. We care a lot about you, and we are worried."

"About what?" I snarked.

"We get that your classes are important to you, and honestly, I'm jealous that you're so good at everything. Top grades, amazing academics, clubs, everything."

"Not to mention how beautiful you are." Stacy sat on the other side of me, her hand running down my long ponytail.

"You're the total package."

"So, then why the intervention?" As if I had to ask.

"You need a social life. You need friends. You don't seem to think so, but you do."

"I have friends," I bit back.

"You have associates or classmates familiar with the same stuff you're studying. They aren't friends. Jesus, you're closer to some of your professors than you are with students your own age."

"I don't see anything wrong with that."

"That's exactly what's wrong. You have that mentality."

I knew I weren't getting out of this conversation unless I pushed to the end. "So, what are you asking me to do?"

"One party. Come to one party with us. No books, no itineraries, just us."

I shook my head and opened my mouth to protest.

"Lauren," Claire said quickly. She scooted closer to me, her arm sliding around mine. "You're not going to turn out like your sister. You have too much control for that."

Her words hit me like a brick. An image of Kat lying on our bathroom floor flashed into my head. It was the last image I had of her.

"I can't do this." I stood up and shook the memory from my head, but they both pulled me back down.

"It's not going to be easy, but you need to do this." As Stacy leaned forward her eyes narrowed. I could almost feel her seeking some shred of vulnerability behind my attempted barricade. "You can't let bad memories destroy your life."

"How is my life being destroyed?" I defended. "I think I'm doing quite well."

Claire didn't seem to think so. "Why did you get into neuropsychology?" she asked. "The study of human behavior and why people do what they do?"

"What?" Her question threw me off.

"It's because you can't get any answers on why Kat died the way she did. Why she allowed all the bad into her life. You are the type of person who needs closure, and I get that. But wrapping your entire life around something because of bad memories is not the way to live a happy life."

"You seem to know all the answers," I said as tears welled up in my eyes. She was right, though.

"I know you aren't happy, genuinely. You soak yourself into the books hoping your answers will be there. But they won't be."

"Claire." I turned toward her to argue her point, but I had nothing. She was right.

"Just one party," said Stacy, plopping onto the floor in front of me. She rested her hands on my knees and looked up at me with innocent eyes.

"What do you say?" Claire chimed in.

"I really can't."

"Why?"

"I don't know."

"If you don't have a good time, we will never bug you again about trying to make friends. We will leave you alone and support you in whatever you feel you need to do."

"One party?"

"We will even let you pick what night you want to go out."

My anxiety level was already up at the thought of putting myself into a situation I didn't want to be in. But, if it got them off my back, I was willing to try.

"Fine," I said, wiping a tear from my cheek. "Next weekend should be fine. I'll plan for it."

"Yay! Saturday night then?"

"Yes." I nodded my head reluctantly, already trying to find a way to get out of it.

"You won't regret it. I promise."

"I already do."

The entire next week went by so slowly, agonizing my brain on the thought of going to some fraternity party with Claire and Stacy. I tried pouring myself into my classes, but my brain kept going back to the what-if-something-happens scenario. I had already made a plan to exit before it got too crazy. My own wine spritzers premixed and poured into a couple of water bottles didn't hold enough alcohol to get an ant drunk so I was good on that aspect too.

When Saturday afternoon arrived, Claire and Stacy couldn't wait to get their hands on me. I was pulled from my room and fussed over until I was wearing the perfect dress with the perfect shades of eyeshadow and lipstick, and my hair was styled to cascade down over my shoulders the way they wanted it to look.

"Perfect," Claire said with a smile.

I looked at my image and didn't recognize the woman looking back. The short black dress and heels were not something I would have chosen to wear. I did have to admit that I liked the make-up. It brought out my features nicely. I tried pulling the hem of the dress down.

"So sexy," Stacy chimed in. "You are going to knock 'em dead!"

"The only thing I'm knocking dead is this notion that you think I need to do this." I pointed at each of them. "Remember, you promised you'd leave me alone if I go."

Claire drew an invisible X over her chest and Stacy nodded excitedly before grabbing my arm and yanking me out of the room.

I only twisted my ankle three times on the way to whatever party they were dragging me to. "Where are we going, anyway?"

"You could say, it's a party in your honor."

"A... what? What did you guys do?"

"Come on." Stacy dragged me up the sidewalk and knocked on a large white door to a large red house with black shutters.

The sun was fading behind us as I tried to listen to any havoc being wreaked behind that door. As it opened, I followed them inside and was immediately offered a plastic cup of beer by a rather good-looking guy with a Sigma Alpha Mu t-shirt on. From my own research, I knew this fraternity was one of the better ones. They did a lot of community work and volunteered their time wherever they could.

"No, thank you. I'm not much on beer. BYOB," I smiled, holding one of my bottles up.

"Well, if you get thirsty the keg is right over there," he smiled, pointing into a corner. "Any one of the brothers or pledges will help you.

"Thank you. I appreciate that."

"I'll take it." Claire snatched the cup from him and took a big drink out of it. "Thanks, Todd." She winked at him before moving into the room further.

There wasn't nearly as many people as I had thought there'd be, but it was okay with me. I opened my drink and took a sip, feeling the tension ease up some.

Claire took my hand and led me inside further. "I guess there is a big party at Delta tonight, so there won't be a lot of people here."

"Bummer," I said, following her toward a group of people lounging on the furniture in the room.

"Everybody," she called out. "This is Lauren, my *other* suitemate. Lauren, this is everybody."

"You have another suitemate?" a male voice called out. "I thought it was just the two of you lovely ladies." The guy was definitely a jock. His entire persona screamed quarterback, right down to the scantily clad female sitting on his right knee and the busty blonde on his other knee.

"Nope. We have a third and we finally dragged her away from her dungeon of a room to show her how the better half lives."

I glanced across the number of faces watching me and forced a smile, half wishing my drink had more alcohol than it did. I glanced at the front door, wondering how soon was too soon to excuse myself.

A strikingly beautiful woman stood up, her eyes locked with mine. She leaned across the coffee table they were sitting around and reached for my hand. "Lauren," she cooed. "You look a little out of place. Come. Sit by me."

I glanced at Claire and Stacy, I guess for approval, before taking her hand. Walking around the table, she moved over from where she initially sat and gave me space to *fit in*.

"I'm Sienna." She leaned toward me, sitting more on her hip closest to me. "Claire told me this was your first party and to treat you good."

"Did she?" I shot her a death glance.

"I love your dress."

I looked down at the basic black dress as her hand ran across my stomach and back again.

"Thanks," I mumbled, discomfort seeping in. For a lack of something better to do, I gripped my drink and took a mouthful.

"What are you drinking?" She was so close to me.

"Um, it's a wine spritzer. Something I made up."

"May I?"

No, you may not, I thought as I handed it to her. I watched her sip it and smile before handing it back to me. "Thanks. It's good."

Claire and Stacy mingled among the group, and the eyes of the others strayed as the newness of me wore off.

"Let's play a game." Sienna perked up.

"Since when do *you* want to play anything?" the jock blurted out.

"You're a guy, Jack. I don't play with guys."

He swung his arm around one of the girls to grab himself in the groin area and shake it. "Play with this tool. You'll never go back to pussy."

"In your dreams tough boy. I know what's good. You're not it."

I chuckled with a new respect for Sienna. I loved her confidence.

"So, I'm in."

I looked across the table at the voice, and I stared. He was beautiful. He didn't seem to fit the fraternity narrative at all. His hair was longer than the others, disheveled but sexy, which told me he wasn't a jock. Black rimmed glasses gave him a hint of intellect and the tone of his arms let me know he was into fitness. He smiled at me and I melted a little.

"That's Mason," Sienna said, leaning into me. "Definitely a good catch if you're into that sort of thing."

"You mean, dick?" Jack interrupted, laughing hysterically.

I leaned back, heat surfacing in my face. I glanced at Mason. Did he hear that too? He winked and smiled at me, and I melted a little more.

"In your dreams, jockstrap. Anyway," she continued, "this game is called Say It or Teach It."

"Never heard of it," said Jack as sarcastically as he could.

"Oh, you will," she grinned. I liked her a little more. "Someone asks you a question. You tell them a story of your experience on the subject. Then ask the same to someone else. If *that* person doesn't have a story, they are taught by someone in the group, giving *them* their first experience."

My stomach knotted and I glanced around at the others. This was not going to go well. I tried standing up without being noticed, but several eyes caught me. "I'm going to find the bathroom. I'll be right...."

Sienna grabbed my arm and pulled me back down. "Not yet," she whispered. "Trust me on this. You don't want to miss it. I'll go first." She cocked her head and looked right at Jack. "Lauren, since you're new here, I'll start with you."

I smiled an embarrassing smile and swallowed hard.

"Have you ever kissed a guy?"

"Yes!" I blurted, excited that I had a story to tell. "Billy Rothenstein. He was my boyfriend in high school. Not a very good kisser but he was really sweet."

The group cooed and chuckled.

"Okay, your turn." She leaned back and smirked.

I thought for a minute, and I was sure I knew what she wanted me to do. I tried choosing someone I thought had a similar experience. "Mason?" He looked artistic, down to earth, up for anything. How would I know? He was honestly the only one in the group I knew the name of, so I went with him. "Have you ever kissed a guy?"

"I have."

I wasn't sure why, but my heart felt like it skipped a beat when he confirmed it.

"A couple of times, actually. But the one I remember? Reynolds Chapman. He was a professor of mine. Taught me a lot." He stared directly at me and his grin captivated me. Tingles formed between my legs.

"What about you, Jack?" Mason asked, his grin spreading across his face.

"Fuck you, man! I ain't kissing no guy!"

"Then you're out." Sienna sat up straight. "Leave." She was curt and as serious as a heart attack.

"You guys are a bunch of fucknuts!" He pushed the two girls off his knees and stood up. "This is lame anyway. I'm outta here." He bounded out of the room, pushing through a group of people by the door, and disappeared outside.

"Wow," I said softly.

"Now that he's gone, shall we continue? Mason. It's still your turn."

"Sienna. I think I know the answer." He pursed his lips and leaned over the table. He nodded his head upward. "Ever kissed a guy?"

She slowly shook her head and leaned over the table, meeting him in the middle. He glanced at me just before they locked lips and a heated kiss was performed. A twinge of jealousy wiggled its way into me, but I pushed it away. I wasn't staying long anyway, and I certainly wasn't interested in any college guys.

"Mmm." She slid her thumb along her lower lip and smiled. "Very nice for a guy."

"Yeah, I am," he teased.

She looked around and rested her eyes on Claire. "Claire. Ever done a shot of tequila?"

"Just last week. A few too many to be honest. What about you, Lauren?"

"Oh, God, no. I don't touch the stuff." I made a face and shook my head.

"Well, tonight is your lucky night."

My eyes widened when I realized what I had just admitted to. "Oh, no. No thank you. I'm not much of a drinker."

"You're playing the game, aren't you?" Sienna leaned into me and put her hand on my thigh. I didn't know what it was about her, but I liked her touch.

I nodded quickly and pressed my lips together. One of the girls had gotten me that shot and held it in front of me. With all eyes on me, I took the small shot glass and inhaled deeply. Closing my eyes, I poured the contents into my mouth, trying to swallow it before my tastebuds had a chance to reject it. The taste of paint thinner filled my mouth just before the burn took over my esophagus and I did all I could do to hold my breath to avoid either coughing violently or throwing it back up.

The group cheered me on, and a few patted my back as if I had just won a gold medal or something. This game went on through the hour with a few more shots of tequila being offered to me as we played. I didn't care as much about getting out of there at that point.

"Claire, it's your turn to ask a question." Sienna smiled at me.

"Okay, Sienna. Have you ever been felt up by a woman?"

"Pfftttt." I waved my hand in the air. "I know this one." My words didn't want to form as easily as they did, but

I gave it a valiant effort. I leaned toward Claire and whispered loudly. "I'm pretty sure she's a lesbian."

Claire burst out in laughter, covering her mouth, and turning away.

"I am. You're right, Lauren. In fact, my last lover felt me up on this very couch." That shut me up. "What about you?" She stared at me. "Ever been touched by a woman?"

My face felt numb. "Um, yeah." I looked away from her and scratched my head. "In school this one time, I um, went to this dance...."

"I think you're lying, Lauren." Sienna slid closer. "Are you lying?"

I nodded but I couldn't look at her.

"That thrills me," she said. "Do you know why?"

I glanced up at her.

"Because I get to be your first." She licked her bottom lip and gazed down at my mouth. She moved closer. The room around me faded away. Just before her lips touched mine, she looked at the others. Every eye was on us. "Not here." She grabbed my hand, pulled me to my feet and before I knew it, she was leading me up a staircase.

"Where are we going?" My head was a little fuzzy, but I kept up with her.

"Someplace a little more private. I want this to be good for you."

She pulled me into a random room at the top of the stairs and pushed me against the wall. I stared into her eyes and wondered if she was actually going to do this. Would I let her?

The warmth of her breath invaded my senses and she smelled like vanilla and mint. Her hands slid up my sides and cupped my breasts, and I remembered wanting to feel nervous and tense, but I didn't. I liked it. Her touch was soft, subtle, but demanding. Her lips brushed mine and the tip of her tongue teased my lower lip until it slipped into my mouth. She covered my mouth with hers and deepened the kiss, stealing my breath and feeding my body that nervous tension I had initially missed. I trembled uncontrollably as her hand slid down my stomach and between my legs. Her fingers massaged me there until I could feel my own wetness through my underwear.

"God, you're so soft," she mumbled through her kisses. "I want you, Lauren." Her mouth grew needy, her hands explored further, her body pressed into me tighter, and my mind wanted to explode.

A knock on the door interrupted our episode. "Are you at least taking pictures?"

I didn't recognize the voice, but it flipped a switch. I needed to get out of there. It was overwhelming.

I tried pulling away, but Sienna stopped me and cupped my face. "Listen. If you ever want to go down this path, let me know. I would love to see you again."

All I could do was nod before pulling the door open and fixing myself before joining the others downstairs. Sienna followed and gave the group a thumbs up.

"I'm gonna be dreaming about this one, y'all!"

They laughed and snickered, but I held my head up.

"It's your turn, Lauren."

I sat down and cleared my throat, looking around the small crowd. "Stacy, have you ever..." *what have I done in the past? Think Lauren.* "...flashed your boobs at a complete stranger?" I sat back with confidence remembering the concert my friends and I attended.

"I have not!" She smiled wide and instantaneously pulled her top up exposing her breasts for the entire room. She giggled and jumped around without a care in the world.

I shook my head. Why did that not surprise me?

"Have you ever had an oral orgasm... Lauren?"

Why is everyone targeting me? I stood back up and tried to invent an experience, but my mind wasn't working. I felt like an amateur and it was getting uncomfortable. "I have not, but I think I'm out. I had fun but I'm going to go."

"Aw, don't go. It's just a game."

"It's not… just a game. But that is neither here nor there. I'm going to… go."

"Wait." Mason jumped up and fumbled to get over to me. "Don't go." He stood in front of me and took my hands in his. "Stay. I like you. I'd like to know more."

"Knowing I'm naïve and immature compared to all of your sexually active friends isn't enough?"

"They are just being idiots. You don't have to play the game. But I would like you to stay."

I nodded, ecstatic that he wanted me there.

"Come here." He led me toward the back of the house and out the back door where a few stragglers hung out on the back deck. The night air was warm and the fact that Mason wanted to know me made me feel giddy. "You're new to this whole social thing, I get it. I was once there too."

"You were not."

"Well, no," he snickered. "But my little brother was. I helped him through it. There's nothing wrong with being innocent. There is something about you, Lauren. I want to help you." His fingers fed through mine and he pulled me closer. "I think you're so sweet." His kiss was so sweet. I didn't want it to end. "I'll get us some drinks and we'll talk, okay?"

I nodded and watched him disappear back into the house. Moments later he was handing me a glass of what he called the house punch. It was good, but strong, so I sipped it.

"Try this." He handed me a small white pill.

"I don't do drugs," I said, pushing it back to him.

"It's not… it's just… it'll take the edge off, make the party a little less suckish. Here, watch." He popped the same pill into his mouth and swallowed it down with a sip of his drink. "It's nothing. Just a little molly."

I watched his eyes. They were kind. Beautiful. I wanted so badly to believe him. I threw caution to the wind and took the pill from him. Without another thought, I placed it on the tip of my tongue and took a drink. He pulled my face to his and kissed me again.

"Are you really that inexperienced with sex?"

I shrugged. "I guess. I mean, I'm not a virgin or anything, but compared to everyone else, apparently I should have been born with a catholic veil on my head."

He chuckled. "You're funny. I like you."

"Thanks." I looked down and picked at the side of my cup.

"I'd love to be your first."

"What?" I stared up at him. "My first what?"

"Back there, your question was, have you ever had an oral orgasm."

"Um." I was speechless.

"I want to be your first."

My first instinct was to tell him no and leave quickly. Hell, if he'd have asked me the moment I got to the party I wouldn't have entertained him with an answer. I would have just left screaming, with arms flailing in the air.

But, in all honesty I was a newbie. There was a lot I didn't know. Where did it say I had to be in a relationship to experience life? The more I talked to him, the more I wanted to. I didn't have to say anything. He pulled me up to my feet and led me off the steps to the ground. We walked through a small, wooded area to a clearing by a small pond. It was calm, serene. He kissed me with more fervor, pooling me in the palms of his hands. I was slowly submitting to this gorgeous stranger and it intoxicated me.

He lowered me to the soft grass beneath us and hovered over me. The heat from his body seeped into me as his mouth explored mine. His tongue jutted out toward mine playfully as his hands worked my dress up to my waist. The occasional brush of his knee against mine. The drag of his fingertips across my bare thigh. The soft-touch he gave to my sex. It all heightened my arousal. Was this even me? Was I actually there underneath this beautiful man?

He pulled his lips from mine and hesitated, watching my eyes. His lips kissed my chin then lowered down until his next kiss was on my thigh. His fingers danced across my panties and he must have felt how wet I was from Sienna, and then from him.

I thought about the night that had already played out. So many firsts for me. A woman's kiss. Her hands on my body. And now.... I looked down at him as he pulled my underwear aside and swirled his tongue around my clitoris. My breath caught. Sensation poured into me. I swung my head upward and took in a deep breath as he pushed his tongue into my folds. His arms wrapped around my waist and he feasted.

My head was spinning. My libido was raging. My body was on fire. I grabbed at the grass beneath me, my hips moving up and down along his face. When I didn't think it could get any better, he slid his finger inside me and slowly withdrew it, only to slide it back in again. Repeating this while his tongue drew a picture around my clit sent me into overdrive. With my mouth gaped open I pushed my fingers into his luscious hair, guiding him deeper, riding his mouth back and forth until an orgasm threatened me. I stopped and held my breath feeling it spread all throughout my insides.

A guttural moan groveled from deep inside my throat. My orgasm slammed into me and seized every muscle I had until it let go and left me breathing heavily on the ground. I dropped my hands from his head and relished in the moment. Complete satisfaction.

He stood over me, his eyes taking in the mess he had made me. He was delicious in the moonlight and I wanted to stay there and soak him in. He offered me his hand and reluctantly I took it. He helped me to my feet, and I adjusted my dress back down to a presentable state.

"Are you okay?" He pulled my face up to meet his.

"I'm more than okay. Who would have thought I would ever do something like this."

"You were incredible."

"I was?" I argued. "You did everything, are you kidding me? Did you go to school to learn that or something?"

He chuckled. "I enjoy giving women pleasure. That's all."

"Well, you're damned good at it. You must have had a lot of practice."

"I've... had my share."

"Have you been with a lot of women?"

"I won't lie," he said, nodding his head. "I've been with several people."

"People.... Meaning?"

"I'm bi-sexual. And I like my sex, a lot."

Arousal poked around again, confusing me. Shouldn't this be a red flag? Why was I this attracted to him, or the idea of what he could give me? Was I bi-sexual as well? I bit my cheek and smirked at the thought.

"I think I really needed this," I said, deep in thought about what I had done.

"Why do you say that?"

"For the first time, I haven't been pressed down about bad memories in my past."

"Do you want to talk about it?"

"No. Not really. I don't want to depress the night."

"Let me guess. I have turned you into a sex addict."

"Would that be a bad thing? "Anytime you want to do that?" I said, pointing back to where he lay me down. "You just let me know. Put me on speed dial, actually."

"Will do," he chuckled. "Honestly, if you like that, and you're up for some crazy shit, I've got some friends who'd jump at the chance to help you out."

A shiver ran through me. I inhaled deeply. "Friends?"

He stopped walking and turned toward me. "A couple of buddies of mine really like to fuck. They do threesomes all the time. No pressure though. I'll be right there if you want me to be."

"What if I said I might be interested?"

"I say I might be able to introduce you."

"Tonight?" There was the old me. Cold feet and ready to run back to my room.

"Only if you want. I know they would love to meet someone like you."

"What does that mean?"

"You're fresh, innocent."

My stomach was in a knot, but my pussy was tingling with excitement, and nowhere was there a bad thought of my past. I was feeling amazing and carefree, and I wanted more of what Mason gave me. "Let's go," I said, smiling wide.

He matched my smile, took my hand, and led me back into the house. He grabbed two drinks on our way into the living room and with a nod from him when he locked his eyes on two guys in the corner, they headed in our direction.

I leaned against the wall with my hands behind my back and tried to control my trembling.

"Hey, man." Mason slapped each of their hands as they approached us. "I want you to meet someone special."

Both of them looked me up and down.

"This is Lauren. She's new to the scene. Lauren, this is Randy and Charlie."

They were both tall and could have passed for brothers, each having sandy brown hair and brown eyes. I waved at them, my lips tight together.

"Lauren is possibly interested in trying a little soiree with us."

"Well, it is *very* nice to meet you." Randy leaned against the wall next to me, his arm over the top of my head.

"I, um.... I have never done anything like this before, but" I bit my lip and he swooped down and kissed me hard. He pushed his tongue into my mouth and dominated the area as his hand gripped my breast.

"That's all she needed to say," said Charlie. "I'll go upstairs and find a room. You have condoms?"

Randy pulled away and licked his lips hungrily. "Always."

"Listen, "Mason said. "Lauren is a sweetheart. Treat her as such. No rough stuff unless she asks for it." His grin was intoxicating.

"You're coming, right?" I pleaded with him.

"Well, I will be soon." He patted my behind and followed me up the stairs behind Randy. Charlie had already disappeared into a room.

I was so nervous; butterflies were fluttering around in my stomach. The moment I stepped into the room I heard the door close behind me. Randy and Charlie stood next to a small bed and they were looking at me as if they were waiting for me to start. I didn't know how. I didn't know what to do.

When I felt Mason's hands on my shoulders from behind, the butterflies went away. His mouth kissed the side of my neck and arousal stirred inside me. I closed my eyes to savor the feeling and when I opened them again Charlie and Randy were both bare-chested. Charlie was unbuckling his pants and Randy was rubbing himself through his jeans, looking at me like I was a piece of meat for his dinner. Another shiver delighted me.

Mason slid his hands down my sides and hooked his fingers under my dress, dragging it back up exposing me. As condoms were being passed out, my dress was being discarded to the side. This was it. I was about to become a slut, and the idea thrilled me. A sex toy for three college guys I barely knew. Somewhere between Mason's hands on my body and the other two disrobing, I lost my bra and underwear. I stood in the middle of them, their cocks protruding forward and their eyes hungry for me.

They closed in and I inhaled deeply, my breathing working a little harder. A mouth kissed my shoulder and worked down to my breast. It covered my nipple and his tongue swirled around the hardening nub causing a sensation to build deliciously. Another mouth bit at my neck while hands groped my ass and slid between my legs. Mason turned my head to kiss my mouth, his tongue teasing as he kept his eyes open to watch my reaction. I wrapped my hands around two cocks and started stroking them, remembering a porn show I watched with my ex-boyfriend one time. I tried mimicking what I saw, and it seemed to work. Moans came from their mouths as their kisses got rougher.

Teeth bit at my ear. "Suck my cock," Charlie whispered.

I got down on my knees in front of him and opened my mouth. The tip ran along my lip as I twirled my tongue around it. It felt natural, like I had done it a thousand times. He slid his hands behind my head and pulled me in, his cock sliding along my tongue until it filled my mouth. I sucked him, bobbing my head back and forth, my arousal surrounding me. I stroked Randy and Mason in each hand imagining what I looked like in their eyes. I worked Charlie harder, wanting to swallow him.

He pressed me in harder and his tip hit the back of my throat. His pubic hair crushed against my nose, but I held him there, my tongue stroking the side of him.

"Fuck," he whispered aloud, pulling out. He thrust his hips back and forth, fucking my mouth. He wasn't a big guy, but I loved the feel of him on my tongue. When he pulled out, Randy directed my head toward him. I hungrily obliged taking him into my mouth and sucking the tip. He was a little bigger, but I was easily able to fill my mouth with his mass. I stroked my lips back and forth along his shaft until he was panting, then I pulled away and looked up at Mason.

"May I?" I asked.

He still had his jeans on, unbuckled, and open in the front. He was so fucking sexy, I wanted him inside me. He stepped toward me and I inched his jeans down over his hips, leaving them mid-thigh. His dick sprung out of his pants and my eyes widened. He was twice the size of both Charlie and Randy and thick. I teased his tip with my tongue until his mouth gaped open. Twirling around him I tasted him on my tongue, and I wanted more. I adjusted my body in front of him and slowly took him into my mouth, filling it only midway up his shaft. He still had at least three inches to go.

"Can you fit me," he teased.

I stroked him with my mouth, preparing myself to try and please him. I pushed him to the back of my throat and tried controlling my gag reflex as he pressed against my tonsils. I pulled him out when I was unsuccessful and tried again. I sucked on him, easing him into my mouth inch by inch until the tip of his cock pushed against the back of my throat. I held my breath and opened my mouth as wide as I could. The feel of his mass stretching my throat as I pushed myself on him exhilarated me and I held him there.

"Oh, my God! Lauren! Yes." His head fell backward, and his hips moved back and forth slightly as he fucked my throat. I pulled back to get a breath and looked up at him. He was in heaven, his mouth gaped open, his eyes full of lust and his cock as hard as steel.

He picked me up off my knees and led me to the bed. He cupped my face and kissed me with fervor. He caressed my back, slid his hands down between my legs, and pushed his finger inside me.

Charlie and Randy came up on each side of me, their hands roaming my body, pinching my nipples, and slapping my ass. Mason slid his jeans off, pulled a condom from his pocket, and without taking his eyes off me, he rolled it on.

"Turn around, Lauren."

My name on his lips was so sexy. I turned around and knelt on the bed, my hands keeping me up off the mattress. Mason's hand ran across my pussy before he grabbed my hips and pressed his cock against me. He moved back and forth only slightly threatening to penetrate me until I was ready to beg him to fuck me.

He opened me and agonizingly inched his way inside me, stretching my pussy around his cock. I had only had sex with one other guy in my life and tonight I was going to fuck three of them. I buried my head into the mattress as the sensation of Mason's cock filling me pushed through every fiber of my being. He began slowly, his dick slick with my juices.

Charlie cupped his hand underneath my chin and lifted me back up to my hands. He sat in front of me, his legs wide. He directed my mouth onto his cock, and I sucked him all the way in. Randy stroked himself next to me while his other hand played with my breast. Each time Mason jarred me forward I pushed Charlie into my mouth as far as it would go, pulling my lips tight, and sliding them back off him until he grabbed my head and started fucking my mouth fast. He was moaning and I could taste him more and more. He shoved himself deep inside and cum filled my mouth. I swallowed him down, sucking his dick until it was clean, and he was limp.

I imagined what I looked like, a sex slut for pleasure, and it pushed me to a fast but very hard orgasm. I pushed back on Mason, my body shaking uncontrollably. He slammed into me several times, his hips slapping against my ass cheeks until he unloaded himself, grunting as he came. Randy took Mason's place once he moved out of the way and entered me easily. He slapped my ass and thrust into me a few times. I felt his thumb on my ass and the pressure was incredible. He teased me there while he rode me. They were somehow conversing amongst each other, because Mason chuckled, and high-fived Randy just before he pulled out and lined his dick up with my other hole.

My eyes widened. I looked up at Mason as Randy slowly pushed into my ass. I wanted to protest. I was scared to try, but I was also so excited and aroused it didn't matter at this point. I was ready for anything. I gripped the bed and tried to relax as much as I could. The further he pushed into me the more excited I got. My pussy was so wet, and I felt another orgasm swirling around me. I pushed back, rocking on his cock until I exploded, burying my head into the mattress.

Randy pulled out and I collapsed onto the bed, sated and exhausted. Mason sat next to me, his cock still semi-hard. He stroked my forehead while Randy and Charlie got dressed.

"That," said Charlie "was fucking insanely good. Thank you, Lauren for an incredible fuck."

"Anytime you're feeling like being a whore again, just give us a shout. We'll make you feel the part."

I nodded, smiling drunkenly at them. They left the room as they put their shirts back on leaving me and Mason alone on the bed. Moments later, my eyes grew heavy, and I fell asleep.

* * * * * *

I walked along the street my head still trying to wrap around what I did a few nights ago. I couldn't decipher my feelings. Was I embarrassed? Was I appalled? No. None of that. I wanted to do it again. The thought of calling Mason entered my mind a few hundred times since that night. Hooking up with him and his friends, I chuckled. Even saying it thrilled me. What was wrong with me? I had skipped my classes two days in a row and my phone was blowing up with texts and calls from my suitemates. Why didn't I care about any of that? My head was still in the clouds, still trying to figure my life out, still wondering where I went from where I stood.

They deserved something. I wasn't being fair. I pulled my phone and texted Claire.

I'm okay. Just trying to figure some shit out. I'll be home tonight.

The moment I sent it I shut my phone off and dropped it in my jacket pocket. I was still wearing Mason's shirt he had somehow put on me while I slept. I did a little shopping and bought some shorts and a toothbrush. That night I'd check out of the hotel I was staying in and go back to the suite.

It was time to get back to reality, even if I wasn't sure what that reality was.

I grabbed a wrap from a deli close by and found a bench in the park to sit at. Nibbling on the wrap, I watched a group of ducks paddling along in a pond.

"Hello." An older man cast a shadow on me, and I looked up at him. "May I?" He gestured toward the end of the bench.

"Please. Make yourself comfortable. I'm going to be going soon anyway."

"You seem troubled. I'm in the mood to listen if you want to unload."

"Unload. There's a perfect choice of a word. I think I'm good. But thank you."

He sat next to me and continued to watch me. His face was striking, bold, kind. "Are you sure? I have a good sense about people. I was walking by and couldn't help but notice you seemed to need someone to talk to."

Maybe it wasn't such a bad idea. He didn't know me. I could tell him everything. I learned that talking about bottled-up feelings helps get you to the end with a better conclusion. I was ready. I turned to him and took a big breath.

"Are you sure you want to hear my problems?"

"More than sure. I like helping people."

"I think I just turned a huge corner in my life, but I don't know where to go from here."

He crossed his legs and stroked his chin like a therapist would do. I thought it was amusing, but I *unloaded* everything to him.

"I've always been the one to pour myself into my studies, trying to keep away from the social scene and the drinking."

"Why is that?"

"My sister was in that scene, too much. It got a hold of her and she died... from an overdose. I found her on the bathroom floor that night and I haven't been able to get it out of my mind since then, until...." I took a big breath. "Until I went to a party with my friends."

"That changed you, how?"

"I met Sienna, and Mason, and Charlie, and...."

"They introduced you to something you were uncomfortable with, didn't they?"

 "They did," I nodded. "Sex. There were a lot of firsts for me that night."

"Tell me."

"My first kiss from a woman. She touched me in places that aroused me more than I could imagine. Mason...." I couldn't say it, not to this man.

"Did he have sex with you?"

"To put it mildly. My first oral, my first with a man other than my ex-boyfriend, my first with three guys at one time. I became something I used to think was taboo. I was a whore, their sex toy, and even now as I talk about it, it thrills me."

"And you no longer allow the death of your sister to dominate your mind."

"Exactly. It was as if the sex was a gateway to my freedom. I don't know what it means, but I have this new outlook on my life, and frankly, it scares the hell out of me."

"Use it, Lauren. Use this new experience and mix it with your past pain."

"Excuse me? How did you know my name?"

"What?"

"You called me Lauren. I never told you my name."

He looked down as if he had gotten snagged in a lie. "Okay. You got me. I'm Steven Pernell, Professor Pernell."

"You're a professor at my college?"

"I'll be your professor during your senior year. I teach Neuropsychology and Human Factors."

"Oh, God." I shielded my eyes from him as my face heated.

"It's okay. I sought you out when you went missing from your classes."

"How do you even know me?"

"You'll be attending my classes. I like to know who my students are the moment they sign up."

"But, that doesn't explain...."

"Students talk. They've been talking about you."

Surprisingly, I was okay with it. I was surprisingly okay with a lot of things.

"Take the pain from your sister's death and use it to your advantage. Take your new sexual awakening and implement that into your life as well. There are a lot of different careers you can seek out after you graduate."

Like a light switch turning on, I knew what I needed to do. "Sex therapy. It's perfect. I can add some sex education classes to my schedule and teach what I love to do in my life." I was beaming with happiness. "Thank you so much, Professor. You don't know how much you helped me."

"I think you helped yourself by stepping out of your comfort zone. You just needed to be turned a little in the right direction. That's all I did."

I hugged him and wanted to scream to the world.

By the time I had gotten back to the suite, no one was there. It was around dinnertime, so the cafeterias were open. I took advantage of the quiet. I went into the living room and spread out on the couch where Claire and Stacy made out the night they intervened in my life. I slid my hand into my shorts and closed my eyes. Thoughts of Sienna's mouth on me sparked my arousal. I moved my fingers around my clit as I remembered what Mason and his friends did to me. I pushed two fingers inside my pussy and slowly moved them in and out until waves of pleasure threatened to dominate me. I worked them a little harder, a little faster, and ran my fingers over my nipple causing my orgasm to slam into me. I bucked my hips up and down moaning and enjoying waves of pleasure crash into me repeatedly. Feeling sated, I made my way to the bathroom, showered, slipped back into Mason's shirt, and sat down at my laptop to make changes to my schedule.

My phone beeped and I pulled it toward me. It was Mason. I smiled and opened his text.

Rumor is you've gone missing. Hope you're okay. I wouldn't want to think I had something to do with it. Would love to see you again. M.

The familiar arousal returned as I responded to him.

*No longer missing. Time to right what was wrong in my life. Celebrate with me this weekend. Bring friends. *winky face*.*